Three Rode Together

Jesse Glover was minding his own business when Ulysses S. Grant summoned him to Washington, asking him to quit the life of a cowboy and keep Arizona safe from the likes of Cochise and Geronimo. So Jesse saddled up and headed for Fort Bowie and its Indian-hating commanding officer, Major Nicholas Calloway.

Along the way he saved a beautiful White Mountain Apache girl named Morning Star from a monstrous fate. And when he tangled with a ruthless gang who was determined to start a whole new Indian uprising, he found help in the shape of two unlikely allies – a Zulu warrior named Sam and a Chiricahua Apache named Goyahkla, who was better known as Geronimo.

Three Rode Together

Steve Hayes & David Whitehead

A Black Horse Western

ROBERT HALE · LONDON

© Steve Hayes & David Whitehead 2012
First published in Great Britain 2012

ISBN 978-0-7090-9631-3

Robert Hale Limited
Clerkenwell House
Clerkenwell Green
London EC1R 0HT

www.halebooks.com

Typeset by
Derek Doyle & Associates, Shaw Heath
Printed and bound in Great Britain by
CPI Antony Rowe, Chippenham and Eastbourne

CHAPTER ONE

The moment Jesse Glover rode over the rise he saw them fifty yards below him.

She was an Apache, with no more than eighteen or twenty summers behind her. He was part-Mexican, part-Indian, and at least a decade older. She wore a beaded buckskin dress and a rawhide band around her head. His red flannel shirt was tucked into well-worn denim pants, his weapons belt pulled low by the weight of a tarnished Frontier Colt. They were struggling with each other in the middle of a shallow, sun-dappled creek, and the half-breed was quickly getting the upper hand.

Jesse reined up.

The half-breed was leaning forward, knees straddling the girl, one big hand grasping her left shoulder, the other clamped across her face. She'd already lost her balance and now lay sprawled on her back in the creek. She tried to kick him off, legs pumping desperately, making the water around her explode like molten silver.

Jesse's mouth tightened.

He usually didn't involve himself in another man's business. Life was simpler that way. But because it was hard to turn a blind eye to rape or maybe murder, he slid his .44/.40 from its scabbard and levered in a round.

The girl finally unbalanced her attacker. He crashed down on top of her. There was a splash – not much of one, because the creek was running shallow this time of year – but the more she kicked and struggled beneath him, the louder he laughed.

There were three of them down there, all told: the squaw, the half-breed who was trying to rape her and a second man, who had left his place by their small campfire and moved closer to the bank to watch the uneven contest.

None of them saw Jesse until he put a bullet into the water next to the half-breed's head.

The impact sprayed a geyser of water over the 'breed's already soaked shoulders. The man on the bank immediately spun around, crouching as he grabbed for his sidearm, a single-action Colt. He was younger, skinnier and taller than his companion, with long, mouse-colored hair and hollow cheeks.

Jesse quickly levered another shell under the hammer, the gesture freezing the younger man in his tracks.

The 'breed in the water sat up, looked around and shook his head to get the wet hair out of his dark eyes. He had the lean face of a hungry wolf, a mottled skin the color of copper, a sharp chin cross-hatched with black stubble.

He wasn't laughing any more.

Jesse slowly walked his golden sorrel down toward them. The campsite was a mean little affair that stank of coffee and beans. Two horses watched him from the shade of a lone juniper, their tails working lazily to keep the flies off. It was summer in Arizona and the day was bright as brass. It was hot, too; as close as made no difference to a hundred degrees.

As Jesse guided his mount around their discarded gear and up-ended saddles, the Apache girl struggled out from under her tormentor and scrambled to her feet. Jesse gave her a quick glance. She was of average height, but that was the only thing about her that was average. In every other respect she was. . . .

'Who the hell're you?' demanded the 'breed in the creek.

Jesse drew rein and looked from the speaker to his companion and back again. They had a look about them he knew all too well. Unless he missed his guess, they were *comancheros*: that low breed of men who traded with the Indians in these parts – the Pueblo and Comanche, Apache, Kiowa and Navajo – providing them with the weapons and ammunition they needed to keep killing the white man, and the illicit firewater that only made them more belligerent.

Once again Jesse's eyes found those of the girl. Her oval face was smooth, framed by raven-black hair that fell to the small of her back. Her large hazel-gold eyes were set above high cheekbones. She had a small, snubbed nose, a cleft chin, and a defiant set to her lips that should have made her look haughty but instead was curiously appealing.

'Just tryin' to figure out what's goin' on here,' Jesse answered softly.

The 'breed swapped a glance with his companion and grinned. 'She said *no*.'

There was a clear mixture of hope and expectation in him that Jesse would grin right along with them and tell the 'breed to carry on teaching that uppity squaw a lesson, 'cause that's all them Indian women were good for.

Instead Jesse said: 'How'd you get her?'

'Bought her.'

Jesse, sensing the 'breed was lying, said: 'Who from?'

'Some miners.'

'Where?'

'Around.'

Again Jesse looked at the girl. 'You belong to these men?'

She shook her head, no.

'You want to stay with them?'

Again, no.

'Then get over here.'

While Jesse was addressing the girl, the man on the bank seized his opportunity. Again he hooked at the Colt high on his right hip and this time had it halfway clear when Jesse's Winchester cracked a second time. The man's legs went stiff. The gun spilled from his nerveless fingers. He corkscrewed to the ground and lay deathly still.

The half-breed in the creek started reaching for his own sidearm, but froze when Jesse pumped the lever again and aimed the Winchester at his heart.

'Don't,' he advised quietly.

The half-breed grudgingly raised his hands.

'You didn't have to kill him,' he said, indicating his fallen companion. 'He weren't much more'n a boy.'

'Should've thought of that 'fore you let him pack a gun.'

'Could'a winged him in the shoulder just as easy.'

'Maybe I could, at that. But it's been a long ride and I'm tired. And when I get tired, my hands shake, mistakes happen.'

8

'That weren't no mistake,' snapped the half-breed.

'No,' Jesse replied. 'It wasn't. Now, you ease that smoke-wheel out *real* careful, mister, finger and thumb only, and toss it away.'

'The hell I will!'

Jesse shrugged and squeezed harder on the Winchester's trigger.

Reading death in his eyes, the half-breed finally did as he'd been told and tossed the six-gun up onto the far bank, well out of reach.

By now the girl had climbed out of the stream. When she was close enough Jesse kicked one foot free of the stirrup and she stepped up into the saddle behind him. She clasped him around waist. It was a nice feeling, he thought, even if she was soaked to the skin. Keeping his eyes on the half-breed, he said: 'Got a name, mister?'

'Quintero.'

'Well, Quintero, I got two pieces of advice for you. First: don't come after us. If you *do*, you'll get an extra hole in your belly you don't need.'

'Second?' Quintero said belligerently.

'Don't bury your friend 'fore you check him out.'

Puzzled, Quintero squinted at him. 'Say again?'

'The boy. Don't be in a rush to put him under.'

Quintero slowly nodded, though he still didn't get the stranger's point.

Jesse gathered the reins, kicked up his horse and rode away.

Quintero angrily watched Jesse taking the Apache girl with him. Then he got up and waded ashore, rapidly turning the bank into mud. There, he stared down at his late partner.

Otis Barstow had been a trial at times, but he'd always been a friend, and real friends were rare in the world they inhabited. Quintero reckoned he'd miss him.

Then Otis groaned and Quintero leapt back as if scalded.

'What in *hell*. . . ?'

Otis sat up, holding his long, narrow head in both hands. Squinting, Quintero looked closer at his scalp. The stranger's bullet had creased it, momentarily knocking Otis senseless, but done no more damage than that.

Don't bury your friend before you check him out, he'd said.

Quintero shook his head and muttered with feeling: '*Hijo de dios*! That was some shootin'!'

CHAPTER TWO

A herd of wild mustangs grazed quietly along a verdant stretch of land between tall, red-rock walls. A minor miracle of nature, the canyon was almost completely at odds with the harsh semi-desert that surrounded it. Its broad floor was covered in lush, emerald-green grama grass, with border piñons and tall Catawba trees growing here and there along its fringes. A rock pool glistened coolly at one end, the water showing olive green beneath the shade of an age-seamed overhang.

The horses, mostly sorrels and bays, numbered eighteen. They ranged in size from fourteen to sixteen hands and were by any stretch magnificent . . . as indeed was the man who patiently watched over them from higher ground.

Standing well over six feet in height, he was naked to the waist, his long legs encased in brown cavalry pants tucked into well-scuffed preacher boots. His chest was deep, his waist tapered, his skin as dark as ebony. Around each muscular bicep he wore a distinctive armlet fashioned from the feathers of a white eagle.

Though peaceable by disposition, he held a short-handled, long bladed stabbing spear known in his own country as an *assegai*. At his belt hung a *bolas* – three rawhide thongs joined at one end, to each of which was tied a smooth, fist-sized rock. His birth-name was almost unpronounceable to the people of this land. Here, if he was addressed at all, folks called him Zulu Sam, and that name was as good as any.

Suddenly Sam tensed and sniffed at the air, his fingers tightening around the assegai as he turned toward the southeast. A dust cloud balanced on the horizon, silhouetting five riders who were approaching at a gallop.

He recognized them immediately, for this was not the first time they'd come seeking horses. He saw the ropes in their hands, bouncing and flipping like dead snakes, and knew they were here to try their luck again.

Out on the flats, the horsemen spotted Sam at the same time and immediately slowed to a halt, for past experience had told them he was not a man to be taken lightly. One of them, short and thin, with a pinched face that matched his spiteful nature, hissed: 'It's that damn' Shadow Horse again!'

Their leader, a large man who went by the name of Cordon, said: 'A month's pay for anyone who brings him down!'

Ropes were quickly replaced by carbines as the riders took off again.

Realizing that he was their target, Sam grimly turned back to the canyon and uttered a shrill sound of warning that was uncannily like the whinny of a horse. At once the mustangs below pricked their ears, then wheeled and started toward the far end of the canyon.

His warning given, Zulu Sam descended to the canyon

floor in a series of effortless bounds and leaps. Tireless, and as sure-footed as any mountain goat, he made it look as easy as descending stairs. He hit the ground at a sprint, came out just ahead of the galloping broomtails and led them toward a narrow defile a hundred yards farther on, which led to open country and freedom.

Though the imminent arrival of Cordon's mustangers was cause for concern, Sam knew that once they made it through the defile they could disappear into the badlands beyond, where hills as red as fresh-spilt blood rose up out of golden sands and age- and heat-twisted pines would give them all the cover they needed to make good their escape.

But this time, Cordon had thought ahead.

As Sam loped tirelessly toward the canyon exit, the herd following as faithfully as if he'd been their lead horse, a sixth member of Cordon's crew, crouched among the rocks above the defile, followed their approach. He held a rifle and his weathered, pocked face was split by a cruel grin.

When he judged the time to be right, he drew a knife from the sheath at his hip and sliced through the length of rope in front of him. The rope had been holding a tree-sized log in place on the rocks at the edge of the pass. Now, the log rolled right over the edge and dropped out of sight.

As it fell, however, its weight acted as a counter-balance that yanked on a second, stouter length of rope to which it was attached. A net that had been carefully hidden beneath a carpet of leaves and sand the night before sud-denly shot up and jerked into position across the defile, effectively sealing it off.

Caught by surprise Zulu Sam pulled up, his shock

quickly turning to anger. Behind him the horses broke stride and started milling in confusion. Then Sam threw himself at the net and started slashing at it with his assegai.

The sharp blade sliced through the rope as if it were taffy. Once it was shredded, he jumped aside so that the herd might continue their escape.

The mustangs boiled out of the canyon in an explosion of dust and sound. Sam was about to follow them when there was a blur of movement to his left. He whirled around, too late as one of Cordon's mustangers rode straight into his path.

Sam switched directions, only to run into a second galloping rider. Sam bounced off the side of the man's horse, dropping his assegai in the process. As he bent to retrieve the weapon he heard more horses coming, and whirled just as Cordon and his two remaining men thundered up.

With no choice now he backed up against the nearest rock wall, drew his bolas and began to swing it threateningly.

In the rocks above him, Cordon's sixth man dabbed spit on the sight of his rifle and took aim. Down below, Cordon caught the wink of sunlight on steel and bawled: 'Hold your fire, Curly! I reckon we'll have some fun before we kill this feller!'

It sounded like a good idea. Grinning, the others tucked their Winchesters away and untied their ropes.

One spun a loop and tried to drop it over Sam's head, but the Zulu was too agile and avoided it. A second rider tried to rope him, but Sam dodged that too. He swung the bolas even faster, then launched it at Cordon.

It spun through the air like a whirling, oversized dragonfly and struck its target dead-on, quickly wrapping itself

14

around the man's exposed throat and choking the life out of him. Cordon reached up and tried to tear the rock-weighted thongs loose. But panic made his movements clumsy and as he struggled he lost his balance and fell from the saddle.

A man named Logan quickly dismounted and hurried to his aid. The others drew their handguns and kept Sam covered, while the one called Curly came scrabbling down off the higher ground to help. Logan deftly unwound the bolas from Cordon's neck and helped him sit up. Gasping, Cordon took in several shaky gulps of air.

'You OK, boss?'

Pale-faced, Cordon croaked: 'Y-Yeah, I reckon.' Then, with a baleful glare at Sam: 'OK – let's string the bastard up!'

Because Sam had been a thorn in their side for so long, the men needed no further urging. Dismounting, they crowded him and tried to wrestle him to the ground. It wasn't easy. He was strong and cat-quick. He fought them off for several minutes, but finally one man tripped him and Sam went sprawling. They were on him instantly, pinning him to the ground. A rain of blows and kicks followed, until Sam was barely conscious. And still they kept it up.

From the opposite rim of the canyon, a small group of Apaches watched the drama with interest. Each of the four warriors was painted for war – black around the eyes, the mask effect underlined by a single streak of white – and carried either a lance, bow, a stolen carbine or a flop-headed club. One of them, Little Wolf, turned to their leader and asked: 'Why do we not help *Haskiiyii-Thii*?'

15

Like Sam, their leader was in his mid-thirties. He had long, thick, center-parted hair held back off his broad face by a war cap with rawhide ears. Beneath his blue cotton shirt and breechclout he was sturdy and powerful, with close-set eyes above high cheekbones. His name was Goyahkla, which in the Chiricahua dialect meant 'One Who Yawns'. But there was nothing sleepy about him now as he watched Cordon's men tie the Zulu's hands behind his back and then drag him, semi-conscious, to his feet.

'It is not our fight,' he said stoically. 'The man-horse is nothing to us.'

'But the *wasichu* are our enemies,' said another Apache, whose name was Runs Slowly. 'We would kill them anyway.'

'Runs Slowly is right,' agreed a young, scarred brave called Blue Crow. 'I say we help *Haskiiyii-Thii* before the White-Eyes choke out his spirit.'

'And I say we will not.'

Blue Crow looked sullenly at Goyahkla and muttered: 'It is what Cochise would do.'

Stung by the remark, Goyahkla glared at him. He was jealous of Cochise and Blue Crow, like all Chiricahuas, knew it. Cochise was older and considered far wiser than Goyahkla, something that ate at him. He had also suffered the loss of relatives, losing his brother and two nephews when a US cavalry officer named Bascom had treacherously invited them to a 'peaceful powwow' and then killed them. Cochise had managed to escape, cutting his way out of the tent in which he was being held, enhancing his already near-legendary status in the tribe.

But none of this mattered to Goyahkla. In his eyes, in his heart, he had experienced an even deeper loss when Mexicans had murdered his wife and children. From that time on Goyahkla's grief and thirst for revenge had never faded and he'd savagely killed Mexicans and White-Eyes whenever he had the chance.

Thus Blue Crow's suggestion that Cochise would engage the enemy where he, Goyahkla, would not was an insult that he could not let pass.

'Then come,' he said coldly.

Without another word he wheeled his mount toward the trail that would take them down to the flats below.

Eager for blood, the other Apaches quickly followed.

CHAPTER THREE

By the time Sam regained consciousness, he realized he'd been dragged from the canyon out onto the plain and boosted up into the saddle of Cordon's horse. The stoutest bough of a ponderosa pine stretched directly overhead, and Cordon himself was standing close by, busily turning his lariat into a hang-rope. As he fashioned the noose he made the work look easy; Sam guessed he'd probably done it before, likely more than once.

A wave of nausea swept through him. He fought back the urge to vomit and gazed about him. Cordon's men were standing a short distance away, smoking and chatting as they waited for the fun to commence. They'd tied their horses to some scrubby brush a few yards off.

It galled Zulu Sam to think that this was how he was to meet his end. Peaceable though he was, warrior blood flowed through his veins. If he had to die at all it should be in battle, or of a ripe old age, but not dangling at the end of a rope; especially since his only crime was to respect the freedom of the horses who'd adopted him.

He strained against the ropes holding his hands behind him, but they'd been tied well. He could still use his feet for kicking, of course, and make this lynching a sight more difficult for them than they'd anticipated. But the end would still be the same. He could measure his life in minutes.

He stared off into the distance, hoping a sense of peace would overtake him. He wanted to take comfort in the fact that the mustangs – the closest thing he'd had to family since the Arabs had forcibly taken him from his beloved Zululand – had escaped. He wanted to feel that his solitary life was no great loss. But that was just horse-apples. All he craved right then was the use of his hands and his assegai. Then he would make sure it was his tormentors who faced death this day instead of him.

Finished fashioning the noose, Cordon stretched up, dropped it over Sam's head and snugged it tight just below his left ear. Sam looked him straight in the eye, showing no fear, just contempt.

Ignoring him, Cordon threw the other end of the rope up over the bough and barked: 'Banham!'

Banham, the small, thin man with the spiteful face that matched his nature, nimbly scaled the tree and tied the rope firmly to the bough. He climbed down again and all of them gathered around to watch Cordon slap his mount on the rump and make it ride out from under Sam.

A curious silence settled across the scene. Cordon and his men had played this cat-and-mouse game of theirs for months now, and yet this was the first time any of them had ever seen Sam up close. The Zulu had a high forehead below his dark, close-cropped hair. His ears were small, his nose broad, and he wore a wispy mustache and forked goatee beard. His eyes were wide-spaced, a little bloodshot now, and the color of amber.

'Got any last words?' Cordon asked him.

Sam stared at him, unblinking.

'I said, you got any last words?' repeated Cordon.

Sam said softly: 'Just one.'

Curious, Cordon frowned, leaned closer and said: 'Spit it out.'

His face suddenly split by a wild grin, Sam yelled: '*Apaches!*'

Even before the word had left his lips a barbed, stone-headed arrow buried into Cordon's spine and slammed him forward against the horse. The animal instinctively reared up and knocked him away, then bolted. A moment later Sam was dangling from the end of the rope, his life being choked away.

The bastards were going to get their hanging after all.

His face bleached white by shock, the man named Logan yelled: 'Injuns! Let's get outta—!'

Goyahkla's lance skewered him and he crashed to the ground.

The others clawed for their guns, shooting wildly over their shoulders as they ran for their spooked horses. Surging across the flats toward them, the four Apaches showed no signs of slowing down.

'Ride, dammit!' screamed Curly, leaping onto his saddle. '*Ride!*'

As Sam continued to kick and struggle, the remainder of Cordon's crew lit out. Moments later the Apaches blurred past the Zulu, yipping at the tops of their lungs as they gave chase. Blue Crow caught up to Curly and, with one swing of his club, caved the rider's skull in.

Nearby, Runs Slow drew rein and fired his Springfield. The bullet missed Banham but hit his horse in the flank.

The creature plunged forward, stumbled and went down with a startled scream. There wasn't much left of Banham when the animal, its neck broken, finally flopped dead on its side.

The two survivors vanished into the badlands, chased only by a rooster-tail of dust.

Returning, Goyahkla drew rein beside the dangling Zulu. Having used his lance on Logan, he now held Sam's assegai in one hand. He used it to slice through the hangrope and Sam fell to the ground, gasping and coughing.

Again Sam tried to break the bonds holding his hands behind him. It was hopeless. He tried rocking his head from side to side to loosen the noose and allow him to breath. No good.

Shadows fell across him. He heard the stamp and blow of winded horses, and a part of him realized the Apaches had returned and were standing their mounts in a circle around him, staring at him as if he were a source of great curiosity.

Goyahkla now leapt from his pony and knelt beside the choking Zulu. They looked at each other for a long moment. The Apache's face was as unreadable as Sam's had been just moments before. Much as Sam didn't want to beg, he knew there was a plea in his eyes that he could not suppress. Still Goyahkla looked at him, unmoved.

Then there was a brief flick of motion and a flash of steel as the assegai sliced through the ropes holding Sam's hands behind him. At once he scrambled to his knees, tore the noose from his throat and flung it aside. Fresh air had never tasted sweeter.

Goyahkla scowled at him, the assegai still clutched in his hand. Sam returned the Apache's glare, suddenly

21

wondering if he had only delayed death this day and not cheated it altogether.

Then Goyahkla cracked a rare smile. And behind him, the other Apaches – all young bucks, Sam realized dimly – grinned as well.

When the Chiricahua warrior handed him the assegai handle first, Sam saw no reason not to grin right back.

CHAPTER FOUR

With the creek well behind them, Jesse looked back over one shoulder and said: 'You speak English?'

To his surprise the Apache girl replied with: '*J'ai appris l'anglais de mon père!*'

He reined up and turned to get a better look at her. 'Who taught you to speak French, girl?'

'My papa,' she said, this time in passable English. 'He spoke many tongues.'

'What was he, a schoolteacher?'

'An artist,' she replied proudly. 'From a place far to the east called New Orleans. He travelled to many places to paint what he saw.'

Jesse hid his surprise and kneed his horse to get it moving again. 'That how come he met your ma?'

Behind him, he felt her nod. 'He painted her many times. And each time he fell more in love with her . . . until, finally, she owned his heart and he could not leave.'

'I do like a happy endin',' Jesse admitted. 'Restores your faith in human nature. Where're your folks now?'

'Both are dead.'

Even though he couldn't see her face, he could hear

her voice and knew both had hardened.

'The *comancheros* came at dawn this morning,' she went on. 'I was at the stream, bathing. At first my friends thought it was Comanches – they have raided us before, many times – but I knew better. Only the White-Eyes have so many bullets to waste.'

'What happened?' Jesse asked.

Her voice was dead now. 'They attacked my village, killed everyone that they had no use for. Men, children, the old ones ... I watched them from hiding. I did not know what to do until I saw two of them grab my mother, Pale Fawn. Then I broke cover and threw myself at them, with murder in my heart.'

She twisted around so that she could look off into the distance. The view was desolate; mostly flat, shrub-dotted grassland stretching to every distant horizon, relieved here and there by the occasional piñon or yucca.

'I could not fight them both,' she continued. 'Soon they bore me to the ground. My mother tried to help me. She picked up a rock and would have smashed their heads, but the one you shot killed her.'

'I'm sorry for your loss,' Jesse said. It was all he could think to say. Then, looking around uneasily: 'What, uh, happened to the other *comancheros*?'

'They split up. They always split up when they have finished their butchery and then return to their stronghold by a number of different trails. It makes them harder to track down. Not that anyone would bother. Who is to care if Apache girls are stolen away and sold into slavery south of the border?'

Jesse sighed softly. He'd been lucky there had only been two of them to deal with when he happened along. Had there been any more he might have thought twice before interfering, and that wouldn't have sat well with him at all.

'And your pa?' he asked. 'Was he killed as well?'

'He died at the hands of the Comanche, countless moons ago,' she said. 'They did not want their souls captured by his canvas.'

'Then you've got no one?'

'I *need* no one.'

'Maybe not. But just the same I'll take you to the Indian agent when we reach Fort Bowie. He'll help you find some other White Mountain Apaches to live with.'

'How did you know my people are White Mountain?'

'By the pattern of your beads.'

She absently felt the beaded front of her dress. 'You have sharp eyes for an *indaa.*'

'It's how I stay alive.'

She said, as if thinking aloud: 'My people have a saying: A white man sees with his nose and smells with his eyes.'

'I've heard that saying,' Jesse said. 'And I know plenty of white men that it fits. But there's some it doesn't – as you'll see when you're at Fort Bowie. There's men there – Indian fighters mostly – who can track a snake over rocks and sniff out water in a sun-fried desert.'

She was silent for a few moments. Then, 'And you,' she inquired quietly. 'You are an Indian fighter?'

'I'm many things,' Jesse said, 'most of which ain't important.'

'I did not mean to offend you.'

He chuckled drily. 'You didn't. You hang around army posts long enough, girl, you get a skin like an armadillo.' They rode on for a while in silence. Then, as the thought hit him, he said: 'I didn't think of it before, but if you don't want to go back to your people you can always stay at the fort.'

'Why would I want to do that?'

'Well, might be I could find you work at the trading post.'

'I am an Apache!' she said contemptuously. 'Apaches do not serve others.'

'Now I've offended you.'

He waited for her to say she wasn't offended, but when she remained silent he left her alone.

They rode on, the sun scorching their necks.

Given that he had come to her rescue, she knew she should not have been so hard on him. But her heart was still aching; the feeling of loss was strong in her.

She remembered the first moment she'd seen him, sitting his horse with rifle in hand. He was tall and muscular, the hair beneath his low-crowned gray felt hat black and shaggy at the nape. He wore a blue placket shirt tucked into wool pants, the seat reinforced with buckskin. Knee-high boots, worn without spurs, completed the picture.

And his face; it was regular, worn, stubbly now but usually clean-shaven. His eyes were blue as a summer sky and set deep in his head. His nose was a tad too long but straight, his mouth wide, lips thin. She guessed he had seen about thirty summers, maybe a little less.

After a while she said: 'Thank you.'

'For what?'

'Those *comancheros*, they were determined to—'

'I can guess what they were determined to do,' he cut in.

'I would not have let them,' she said darkly. 'I would

have found some way to kill them first.'

He thought it far more likely that they'd have killed *her* first, but decided to keep that to himself.

'I wish you had killed them both,' she added.

Again he made no direct reply. There'd already been enough bloodshed in these parts as it was. It was one of the reasons he was here now.

Finally he said: 'Name's Jesse Glover, by the way. You can call me Jesse.'

'I am Morning Star,' she replied, and like a lovelorn fool he told himself that the name was as beautiful as the girl it belonged to.

CHAPTER FIVE

When they were well into the rock-strewn foothills to the northwest, Goyahkla called a halt and they let their horses blow. It had been a good morning's work after all, and he was pleased. They were now four horses richer, and had stripped the man Cordon and his three dead companions of everything they could use, especially guns and ammunition. They would return to Cochise's stronghold in triumph.

Runs Slowly broke out strips of beef jerky and they sat in a rough circle to eat. As they did so, Zulu Sam eyed his captors carefully. It had taken him a while, but he'd finally recognized Goyahkla. While the rest of the Apache nation knew him by that name, just about everyone else knew him by another – Geronimo.

Geronimo had first come to prominence after Mexican soldiers had raided his village and killed his wife, mother and three children a decade earlier. At the behest of his chief, Mangas Coloradas, he'd joined forces with Cochise and gone on to carve himself a reputation as one of the most feared Indians who ever lived.

Charismatic and seemingly indestructible – legend had

it that he'd survived numerous wounds during his war against the white man – he'd quickly attracted a large following. Though he wasn't a chief, he might just as well have been, for Sam had heard that his supporters would follow him straight into hell if they had to. Now, looking at Geronimo's excitable young companions, he believed it.

Geronimo leaned back on his elbows. He had been studying Sam, too – though not openly. And because it was bad manners to ask a question outright, he said simply: 'Today I saw a man run with wild horses.'

'Do you think he was pretending to be a horse?' asked Blue Crow.

'It is rude to ask such a question,' chastised Little Wolf, adding: 'But it would be good to know the answer.'

Relieved just to be alive, Zulu Sam was amused enough by this peculiar show of social etiquette to play along. 'Maybe this man prefers horses to humans,' he said.

'It would be interesting to know why,' Geronimo remarked to no one in particular.

' 'Cause horses don't care what color a man's skin is,' Sam replied, 'or if he was once a slave.'

'Apaches not care, either,' said Runs Slowly.

'But sometimes Apaches *eat* horses,' Geronimo reminded them with the faintest hint of mischief. 'Such a man would be wise to decide what he is.'

Sam was about to join in the laughter when there suddenly came an ominous whirring sound from someplace behind Geronimo. At once silence fell, for there was no mistaking the sound for anything other than what it was – the warning rattle of an angry snake.

Geronimo moved his head fractionally. Peripherally he saw that a four-foot, gray-brown diamondback had slithered out of some nearby rocks and was just inches away from his right forearm. As he watched it reared up, ready to strike should it be shown any hostility.

Swallowing hard, Little Wolf started reaching slowly for his club. 'I will—'

'You'll be *still*,' hissed Sam.

Keeping his eyes on the snake, he eased forward until he was on his knees before it. Then he began to move his hands slowly, sinuously and to croon softly. As the others watched, wondering what manner of magic the man-horse, *Haskiiyii-Thii*, was about to perform, the snake's whirring brown and ash-white tail slowed and then . . . stopped.

Still making that strange, low crooning, Sam reached out and gently stroked the rattler's flat head. To the amazement of the Apaches, the snake allowed him to do it. At last Zulu Sam placed his forefinger and thumb just behind the snake's jaws and carefully picked it up. Holding it in both hands, he carried it back to the rocks and gently placed it in shade.

As one the Apaches released their breath.

'The mustangs taught you well,' Geronimo said after he found his voice again.

'I didn't learn that from the mustangs,' Sam said, returning to the circle. 'I'm from a place a long ways from here, called Zululand. Before the Arab slave-traders stole me away from my family, my father was a witch doctor for the Great Elephant Shaka, king of all the Zulus. Like the Apache shamans, he knew about the mysteries of natural medicines and the ways of animals. He passed them on to me.'

His companions looked at him with fresh interest. 'I would hear more about this,' said Geronimo. 'You will ride

30

with us to Cochise's stronghold?'

Sam eyed him steadily. 'As your prisoner?'

'As a *brother*,' said Geronimo.

'Would Cochise allow that?'

'Of course. You are no stranger to us, man-horse. Cochise has seen you before, as we all have. For many seasons we have watched you running free with the mustangs.'

'And I've seen you too, and been grateful you never crossed me.'

Geronimo shrugged. 'Our only fight is with the White-Eyes.'

'Well, I got no problem with that. I don't have much love for the white man either. For years they kept me in chains, making me work for food I couldn't eat and straw that wasn't fit to sleep on.'

Little Wolf said: 'It reached our ears that all slaves were set free after the big war between the white soldiers.'

'I heard that too,' said Sam. 'But I escaped before the Civil War ended, came right to Arizona and hid out with the mustangs. So I never had a chance to be set free legally.'

'Some men would have returned to their own people,' remarked Blue Crow.

'I thought about it,' confessed Sam. 'Then I remembered how many times my belly emptied out during the long voyage here and ... well, a man can only suffer the loss of his family once. To be stolen from them again, for any reason, would be more than I could take.'

It was a feeling Geronimo could understand only too well. 'You will come, then?' he repeated. 'To the stronghold?'

31

'As a brother? Goyahkla, it would be an honor.'

'Good. And if you decide to stay, you will teach me how to speak to the snake that rattles?'

'It would be my pleasure,' Sam said.

'Then from this moment forward, *Haskiiyii-Thii*, you are an Apache.'

CHAPTER SIX

Situated at the far end of a single main street lined with stores, saloons and a hotel, Fort Bowie was an orderly sprawl of low adobe buildings surrounded by a low, white-washed stone wall. More of a military outpost than a fort, the regimental standard of the Sixth Cavalry clung limply to a tall pole at the center of the parade ground, for the late afternoon was hot and breezeless.

Drawing rein at the gate, Jesse scanned the place. Weary soldiers went about their duties, fetching, carrying, chopping or sawing firewood and carrying out post clean-up. The company barracks, enlisted men's kitchen and mess hall had all been built along the eastern wall. Officer's country – the CO's quarters, adjutant and offi-cers' quarters, kitchen and mess, plus married quarters, a modest hospital and guardhouse – lay directly ahead, on the far side of the parade ground.

Reining the sorrel to a walk, Jesse headed directly for the CO's quarters. A trooper standing guard there watched them come with a Springfield .45/.70 canted slantwise across his chest. When they were almost to the hitch-rack the sentry stepped out from under the shade of the porch overhang and issued a challenge.

'Stop right there!'

Jesse brought the sorrel to a halt. He understood the soldier's reaction. He'd been on the trail for a while now and badly needed a bath, shave and haircut. His clothes were caked with dust and he reckoned they could stand as much of a laundering as the man inside them.

'I've got business with your commanding officer,' he said.

The sentry was a freckle-faced redhead with almost invisible eyelashes. 'That you may,' he allowed. 'But you can't bring that squaw in here.'

'Why not?'

'Major's orders. No Indians. Says they stink the place up.'

Behind him, Morning Star said softly: 'I will wait outside the gate.'

Jesse ignored her. 'Step aside, soldier,' he said.

The sentry firmed his jaw. 'Mister, I can't do that.'

Without warning Jesse dug his heels into his horse and it leapt forward. Instinctively the soldier spilled backwards, his temper flared and he started to swing his Springfield around. Jesse moved faster. His Peacemaker suddenly appeared in his hand, stopping the sentry in his tracks.

'Easy, soldier.' Then, as the sentry froze: 'What say we start again?'

The sentry was about to issue an angry retort, but before he could say anything the door to the CO's quarters swung open and a slim young man with a steer-horn mustache the color of tobacco stepped out into the sunlight.

'What's going on here?' he demanded.

Jesse and the sentry both turned their attention to him. He was tall and square-shouldered, with an equally square jaw and incisive green eyes. A single gold bar sewn to the shoulders of his blue uniform blouse identified him as a lieutenant.

'Little misunderstanding is all,' said Jesse, holstering his Colt.

The sentry said: 'I told him the major don't allow no Indians in there, Lieutenant, and—'

Without taking his eyes off Jesse the lieutenant snapped: 'Get back to your post!'

'But—'

'Just do it, soldier!'

While the sentry offered up a grudging salute and did as he'd been told, the lieutenant looked at Jesse, took a longer look at Morning Star and then said: 'I'm Lieutenant Alexander Travers. What's your business here, mister?'

'My name's Glover,' Jesse replied. 'As for my business, I reckon this ought to explain it.'

He took a dog-eared envelope from his shirt pocket, leaned down and passed it to Travers. The lieutenant took it with a frown, then opened the envelope, took out the letter inside and scanned it quickly. A moment later he looked up again and said softly: 'Is this some kind of joke?'

'If it is,' Jesse replied, 'I don't hear anyone laughin'.'

Travers tapped the page with his finger tips. 'But this says the President himself sent you here.'

'He *did*.'

He felt Morning Star tighten her grip on him. He didn't complain.

Travers, meanwhile, chewed his top lip with his lower

teeth. He didn't know whether to believe it or not, but it certainly *looked* official.

'Well, Lieutenant?'

'You, uh . . . you'd better come inside, Mr Glover.'

Jesse dismounted, then turned and helped Morning Star down from his horse.

The lieutenant immediately shook his head. 'I'm sorry – not her.'

Jesse sighed. 'Let's make this real simple, shall we?' he said wearily. 'If the girl doesn't come inside, *I* don't come inside. And since I'm here on official business at the personal request of the President himself. . . .'

He didn't need to finish. 'All right, all right,' Travers said hastily. 'But you'd better let me prepare the major first.'

He vanished back inside the low adobe building behind him. When he came out again, Jesse had tied his horse to the hitch-rack and Morning Star was trading scowls with the freckle-faced sentry.

'Major says it's all right. . . .'

'I kind of thought he would,' Jesse said.

The lieutenant took them inside, across a neat anteroom into a small but tidy office. A Colonial model stove sat in one corner, its thin chimney disappearing through the low ceiling above it. In the opposite corner sat a heavy, clutter-free desk. Behind it, still holding Jesse's letter of introduction in one hand, sat a heavyset man with oiled black hair. He was in his forties, and his pale, jowly face held dark, hostile eyes.

'You'd be Calloway,' said Jesse as Travers closed the door behind them.

The commanding officer of Fort Bowie rose to his feet,

pointedly ignoring Morning Star. 'I am Major *Nicholas* Calloway, yes,' he said, his tone almost as stiff as the stand-up collar on his impractical uniform frock-coat. 'You've already met Lieutenant Travers, I believe. You may speak freely before him.'

'Thanks.'

Major Calloway slumped back into his chair without inviting his guests to do likewise. 'Now,' he said, 'according to this, uh, communiqué, I'm to assist you all I can, so you clearly carry some clout. But exactly who are you, Mr Glover?'

'I'm the man President Grant's chosen to make peace between the whites and the Apaches.'

For just a moment then he recalled his one and only meeting with Grant in the Oval Office. The so-called hero of Appomattox had stared at him from out of that worn, inscrutable face with its high forehead, close-set dark eyes and neatly trimmed gray-black beard, and smiled gently at Jesse's reaction to his little proposition.

'*Why me, Mr President?*' Jesse had asked.

Ulysses Simpson Grant had only been president for a few months, and was determined to finally heal old wounds and put the country – all of it – on a more united footing.

'*Because I hear you like the Indian, my boy,*' he'd replied. '*And more importantly, you understand what makes the red man tick. If you didn't, you wouldn't count Sitting Bull among your friends, and I wouldn't be asking you to quit the life of a cowboy in order to make Arizona safe from the likes of Cochise and Geronimo.*'

'And what is it that you want from me?'

Calloway's question brought Jesse back to the present.

'Cochise is holed up somewhere in the Dragoons, Major. I need someone to guide me to his stronghold.'

Calloway gave a tight, humorless smile.

'Did I say somethin' funny?'

'Not funny,' replied Calloway, 'but hopelessly naive. You see, no one knows exactly where the stronghold is. And even if they did, they wouldn't take you there, Glover, because the Apaches would catch you and them and then torture you to death long before you got there.'

'Even under a flag of truce?'

'Flag of. . . ?' The major shook his head in despair and reached into a glass-topped humidor for a fat cigar. 'I'll be straight with you, mister. You Indian-lovers make me sick. You act like the Apaches are human beings just like you or me. They're not. They're vermin. *Worse* than vermin. They're the Devil incarnate. And the sooner everyone realizes that, the better off we—'

'Morning Star's an Apache,' Jesse reminded, indicating the girl. 'She don't look like vermin to me. Or the Devil.'

'You're welcome to your opinion,' returned the major. 'Let's just hope we don't have to bury you with it. Now, I'll happily supply you with a map of the territory. But from there out you're on your own. See to it, Lieutenant.'

'Sir!' snapped Travers, promptly leaving the room.

'Anything else, Mr Glover?' asked the major.

'Uh-uh,' Jesse said. 'Reckon you've made yourself clear enough.'

Lieutenant Travers was waiting for them in the anteroom with a map of the territory. As he handed it over, Jesse nodded toward Calloway's office door and said: 'He's a mite touchy about Indians, isn't he?'

Travers walked them out onto the porch. 'Don't be too quick to judge him, Mr Glover,' he said. 'His younger brother was killed in a raid on a stagecoach station up in Colorado about six months ago. He was on his way to take up a post at Fort Wallace when a mixed party of Sioux, Cheyenne and Arapaho hit them and killed every man, woman and child at the station.'

Jesse absorbed the news and sighed. 'I can appreciate his pain. There's been too much killing on both sides.'

'Of course. But what makes it worse for the major is the fact that his brother was not unlike you. He wanted to give the Indians the benefit of the doubt, make peace with them. I only met him once, but I think he might just have done it, too. For sure he would have made an excellent army chaplain.'

Jesse held up the map. 'Well, thanks for this.'

'Personally, I wish we could do more. But before you set out, ask around town for a man named Ethan Patch. He's our chief of scouts, a taciturn man but one who knows his job. You can't miss him – he's as tall as those mountains you're headed for and just about as weathered. The least he might be able to do is point you in roughly the right direction.'

'I'll remember that,' said Jesse, and shook hands with him.

CHAPTER SEVEN

'He is a man I would walk many miles not to meet,' said Morning Star as Jesse helped her mount up.

'Don't rush to judgment, girl. He's still mighty young and—'

'I meant the major, not the lieutenant.'

'Ah,' said Jesse. 'Now there's a different story.' He took the reins and led the sorrel and Morning Star back toward the gates.

'Then you do not like him either?'

'Let me put it this way,' Jesse said. 'Had me some tin soldiers when I was a boy. One day I lost one. Looked everywhere for him, but I couldn't find him.' He glanced back at the fort and grinned at her. 'Reckon I just did.'

She returned his smile. But there was sadness in it, and he reminded himself that her world had been turned upside down this morning, and that the loss of her mother and her people was still fresh in her mind.

The fort fell behind them as they walked slowly along Main Street. 'You hungry?' he asked as they passed a restaurant.

She shook her head.

'Anythin' else I can get you? Anythin' you need?'

'No, thank you.'

At last they reached a cleared area on the outskirts of town where a squat L-shaped building had been erected from mud-chinked logs. Outside, a group of ragged-looking squaws and young children stood in line beneath the still-fierce late-afternoon sun. They were lean with hunger and broken-spirited.

A sign above the door read:

> FORT BOWIE TRADING POST
> CALUM TODD
> INDIAN AGENT

Slowing his pace, Jesse looked at the Indians and then frowned at Morning Star. 'Navajo?' he asked.

She nodded.

'Can you speak their lingo?'

'A few words.'

'Ask 'em what they're waitin' for.'

Morning Star slid down off the sorrel and went over to the Navajo woman at the head of the line. They spoke briefly. Then a fat but powerfully built man of about fifty appeared in the doorway, growled a few words to Morning Star and gestured impatiently that she should be on her way.

Bristling, Jesse immediately came closer, looped his reins over the tie-rail out front and said: 'You got a problem here, mister?'

The man fixed him with close-set brown eyes. He had a fringe of hair around his otherwise bald head that was the same shade of red as his full beard. His lips were clamped

41

tight around the stem of an old corncob pipe. As he came forward to meet Jesse, his belly strained at the seams of his striped half-placket shirt and the waist of his blue corduroy pants.

'I do when I hear these heathens spoutin' lies about me,' he said in a hard Scottish brogue.

Jesse looked at Morning Star.

She said: 'These people are waiting for food and blankets. They say that this man Todd promised they would have both, many days ago. But as usual, he sells everything to the miners in Apache Hills, and the Navajo get nothing.'

The Indian agent, Todd, puffed himself up and plucked the pipe from his mouth. 'See what I mean, laddie? Lies. Nothin' but lies!'

'Why would they lie about somethin' like that?' Jesse said.

' 'Cause Apaches always lie, laddie. Makes people feel sorry for them, don'tcha know?'

'These are Navajo,' Jesse pointed out.

'Same meat, different gravy,' Todd countered glibly. 'They're all strangers to the truth.' He stuck the pipe back between his lips and thrust out his big right hand. 'But there's no reason why we whites canna be friends. I'm Calum Todd, as ye've doubtless already guessed. What can I do for ye?'

Jesse shook hands with him, more out of diplomacy than anything else. 'This here's Morning Star. Her village was wiped out by *comancheros* early this morning. Any chance you can see she gets settled with people of her own tribe?'

'And what might that be?'

42

'White Mountain.' He reached into his pocket and drew out a fold of bills. 'I'll pay you for your trouble.'

'You dinna have to pay me, laddie,' said Todd, but he took the money anyway. 'It's my job, don'tcha know. But if it'll make ye rest easier. . . .' He looked at Morning Star. 'Come on inside wi' me, lassie. You look like ye could use a little freshenin' up.'

Morning Star didn't move. Her large, hazel-gold eyes remained fixed on Jesse. 'I want to go with you,' she said quietly.

He'd have been proud to have her along, too, except for his present mission. To Todd he said: 'Give us a minute.'

The Indian agent nodded, turned and re-entered his trading post, scratching his fat backside as he went. Jesse watched him go, noting the cold looks the Navajos gave him as he passed.

Turning to Morning Star, he said: 'I'm sorry. But the last thing I need right now is a woman taggin' along, 'specially a pretty one. I got work to do – dangerous work, like as not.'

'But I could be of help.'

'How?'

'I know Geronimo.'

Jesse frowned at her. 'You're just sayin' that, ain't you?'

'No. As children we played together. His tribe, the Bedonkohes, and my people often hunted together.'

'That mean you can lead me to Cochise's stronghold?'

'No. But I'm sure I would be welcome once we got there.'

'And if you weren't? No, thanks, girl. You've had your fill of trouble. I'm not about to pile on any more.' He

43

grasped his reins. 'I'm sorry, Morning Star. I appreciate that you want to help, but. . . .'

She turned away from him. 'You had better go, then,' she said frostily.

Knowing there'd be no reasoning with her at the moment, he nodded and mounted up. 'I should be back in a week or two,' he said gently. 'I'll look in on you then.'

Not giving her the chance to argue about it, he turned the sorrel around and rode back into town.

CHAPTER EIGHT

Even though he hadn't known her a single day, Jesse was amazed at just how bad he felt about saying goodbye to Morning Star. He told himself it was because he'd saved her from the *comancheros* and felt a responsibility toward her. But more than likely he was just being foolish; after all, women and foolishness had a habit of going together where he was concerned.

Still, he had to put her out of his mind, at least for now. He had work to do: important work. So he stabled the sorrel and booked himself a room at Fort Bowie's one and only hotel, then went out and bought enough supplies to see him through the next two weeks he expected to spend on the trail, plus a pack-mule to carry them. He figured to leave town at first light next morning.

By the time he was finished it was close on dusk and he was hungry. He ate a passable meal of fried chicken and boiled potatoes at the restaurant, and washed it down at the Ace High saloon with a glass of sudsy beer.

The saloon was a single dark room with a low, tobacco-stained ceiling and two wagon-wheel chandeliers. The patrons at this early hour were a fairly even mix of towns-

45

folk, miners in from the diggings at Apache Hills and off-duty soldiers.

As he drank, he had no illusions about the impossibility of the task President Grant had set him. It was a fact of life that some things just weren't meant to get along, like cats and dogs and, all too often, men and women. It was like that with white men and Indians. They'd been killing each other for years now and still hadn't managed to find a way to live together in peace.

And yet, who was to say things couldn't change? All at once he saw Major Calloway's attitude as a challenge, and relished the chance to prove that overweight blowhard wrong. All that two opposing sides ever needed was a go-between, someone to get them talking and listening to each other. After that there was no good reason why they shouldn't learn to live in harmony.

Still, there were few things as mule-stubborn as . . . well, mules and men; and his momentary optimism faded again.

The squeak of the batwing doors made him throw a casual glance over one shoulder. His glass stopped halfway to his lips as he saw Ethan Patch come inside. It had to be Calloway's chief of scouts – there couldn't be two men like that in this territory. He was, as Lieutenant Travers had said, a giant of a man, six-seven at least. He wore greasy buckskins and a New Model Army Colt in a leather pouch just below his right hip. He bellied up to the bar a few yards from Jesse and ordered whiskey.

The drink came and Patch tossed it back in a single swallow. Jesse studied his profile for a moment. He guessed the man was about sixty, with skin like cured leather and a big, misshapen lump of a nose that betrayed his fondness for liquor. A shaggy mustache sat along his top lip and long, curly blond hair fell from beneath his flat-brimmed Plainsman hat. His cool blue hunter's eyes viewed the world from out of creased pouches.

Without looking around he suddenly said: 'Are you gonna stare at me all night, friend, or step on over here an' buy me a refill?'

Jesse grabbed his own glass and joined the big man at the end of the bar. He ordered a bottle of Mule Skinner – he'd read the label when the bartender dispensed Patch's first shot – and then offered his hand. 'Name's—'

'Glover,' said Patch, leaning one elbow on the bar and turning to face him. 'Al Travers told me you'd be lookin' me up sooner or later. Thought I'd save you the trouble.'

They shook. Patch had a good, firm handshake. Patch thought the same about Jesse. 'So – you're off to the Dragoons,' said the scout. 'Hopin' to scare up Cochise, I hear.'

'That's the plan.'

'Well, I wish you luck with it. You'll need it.'

'Is he really that hard to find?'

'No one's found him *yet*,' Patch replied. He tasted the whiskey, savoring the sweet blackberry liquor with which it was laced. 'You know them mountains, Glover?'

'Nope. And I prefer it if you'd call me Jesse.'

'They run about twenty-five miles south to east. In some places they're three miles wide, in others about an even dozen. Now, I don't know what kind of area that gives you in square miles, but it's a big one. A *hell* of a big one, when you're lookin' to find one man that don't want to be found.'

'It's not one man, though, is it?' said Jesse. 'I hear

47

Cochise has between two and five hundred Apaches up there with him.'

'I 'spect he does,' allowed Patch, running his forefinger along the damp edges of his mustache. 'But those peaks rise pretty close to two thousand feet at their highest, which means them two to five hundred Apaches'll see you comin' long before you see *them*. An' even if they don't, which ain't likely, that land up there's a natural maze. You've got steep slopes an' sheer drops, deep fissures an' real thick stands of oak an' sycamore. A man wouldn't have to raise much of a sweat to get hisself lost up there – or worse.'

'Thanks for the encouragement,' Jesse replied sourly. 'But I've got to try, Patch.'

'Why? So the President can open that country up to the miners?'

'So he can make peace with the Indians.'

Patch cracked an unpleasant smile. 'I admire you for givin' him the benefit of the doubt, but my guess is he's working more for the likes of them.' He used his glass to indicate a group of four miners who were sitting at a nearby table, playing cards for matches. One of them, a short, heavy man with a round, whiskery face that looked much older than its thirty years, glanced up at them, then used his broken teeth to work an unlit but well-chewed cigar from one side of his mouth to the other.

'There's a king's ransom in gold up there, so they say,' Patch continued. 'Gold, silver, lead, copper, zinc and God knows what-all else. If Grant makes peace with the Indians, the miners'll be free to go up there an' take out everythin' of worth without the need to fret for their scalps. They'll be real happy about that. So will the army an' all the folks in these parts who stand to make money or get jobs out of it. Everyone'll be happy except the Indians, who'll just have to stand by and watch their land get torn apart – again.'

Jesse swallowed more beer. 'Could be right. But not if I can help it. And not if the President can help it, either.'

Patch made a disagreeable sound that could have meant anything.

'I can see how you'd be cynical about that,' Jesse continued. 'But I stood as close to Grant as I'm standin' to you now, and I looked him right in the eye when he asked me to come out here and do what I could to make peace, and he seemed pretty genuine to me. So – can you help me find Cochise or not?'

While he thought about it, Patch poured himself another drink. Finally he said: 'Travers gave you a map of the territory, didn't he?'

'Uh-huh.'

'Got it with you?'

Jesse drew it from his shirt pocket and passed it over. Patch unfolded it on the counter and studied it briefly, scratching at his lantern jaw as he did so. At last he pointed to a spot on the eastern side of the mountains. Jesse noted that it was marked with the words *Mount Glenn*.

'This here's about the highest spot in the whole range,' said Patch. 'If I was Cochise, I reckon I'd hole up there.'

'You *reckon*, or you *know*?'

Patch smiled at him. 'Well now,' he said very deliberately, 'if I *knew* I'd be duty-bound to tell Major Calloway, wouldn't I? I mean, me bein' his chief of scouts an' all?'

'I reckon you would at that,' Jesse replied, returning the smile. 'Thanks, Patch. I appreciate it.'

'Why? You go up there, you'll like as not come back stone-cold dead.'

The smile turned rueful as Jesse raised his glass in toast. 'Like I just said – thanks for the encouragement.'

CHAPTER NINE

As soon as Jesse had gone Calum Todd lumbered outside, took Morning Star by the arm and led her into the store to his own quarters at the back of the L-shaped building. The dim, jumbled store smelled of flour and lard, beans, pepper, dried fruit and coffee. There was a counter, a cracker barrel, a red coffee grinder, the stump of a tree that served as a chopping block and an upturned water barrel that served as a makeshift table surrounded by four ladderback chairs. Floor-to-ceiling shelves lined every spare yard of wall space, and held a bewildering array of items, from tin cups and coffee pots to plug tobacco, blankets, socks, straight boots, preserves, folded shirts and bottles of Balm of Childhood.

It appeared that Todd also used his dark, cramped quarters as an inventory room, for it was equally jammed with boxes of pressed soap, ladies' shoes and bolts of orange cloth. A narrow bunk ran along one wall, a small table stood before a black pot-bellied stove. A half-empty bottle of Old Overholt sat on the table, next to a smeared shot-glass.

Todd gestured to the stove and told her to get a fire

going, so she could heat some water and take a bath. He said he had a tin tub out back that he'd bring inside for her.

'I am clean enough,' she replied. 'I only bathed this morning.'

Though he was disappointed, he only shrugged. 'Suit yerself, lassie. There's food in yonder pie-safe, iffen you get hungry. Me, I got ma business to tend, but I'll be back to see how you're gettin' along as soon as I'm able.'

The rest of the afternoon passed slowly. She sat in one of the two creaky chairs, dozing as she half-listened to the comings and goings in the store, and thought about her mother, Pale Fawn. It was hard to accept just how completely her life could have changed in such a short space of time. Now everything she had ever known was just a memory – her mother, her friends, her people, her way of life. Even *Scan-To*, the name she'd secretly given Jesse for the color of his eyes.

The sun dropped lower on this day that she would never forget. Shadows lengthened across the unswept floor and thickened in the dusty corners. At last she heard Todd bolt the front door of the store and listened to his ponderous tread as he walked toward the little room he was pleased to call home. He filled the doorway for a moment and stretched his back, then looked down at her and said, around his corncob pipe: 'Hungry yet?'

She shook her head.

'Me neither. Later, perhaps.'

Closing the door behind him, he crossed over to the box that served as his bedside table and lit the Argand lamp there. The room grew marginally brighter but certainly no cheerier. He dropped into the chair on the other side of the table and poured himself a drink from the whiskey bottle. 'So,' he said. 'Ye lost your folks this mornin', eh? Too bad, lassie. Life can be hard enough in these parts as it is. Harder still for a bonnie wee thing like yoursen. Lassie like you needs protection in a harsh land like this.'

Still Morning Star said nothing.

He sipped his whiskey. 'Now, if a wise wee gal had any sense,' he continued, 'she'd ally herself with a man who could take care of her, give her nice things, clothes, gewgaws an' the like. Ye know what I mean when I say *ally*?'

She nodded.

'Aye,' he continued expansively. 'A lassie like that could have a comfortable life out here, with the right man to take care of her. Of course, she'd have to . . . cooperate with that man; show her appreciation, like. That'd only be fair. But in return . . . well, she could live like a princess.'

At last Morning Star broke her silence. 'And if she did not want to live like a princess?'

'*All* lassies want to live like princesses. Smart ones, anyway.'

'I do not.'

His smile faded. 'Well, Morning Flower or whatever your name is, I can promise ye that ye'd find it infinitely preferable to the alternative.' He sat forward suddenly, and instinctively she pushed herself back against her seat. 'Y'see, just as a man can protect a woman an' give her all the things in life that make that life *agreeable*, so too can he take them all away and make that life sheer bloody hell. A wise gal, she'd know where she's well off an' show her gratitude to her benefactor.'

She eyed him levelly. 'You have taken money to see that

I find a home among my own people. You will do that, or you will repay the money and I will leave.'

'An' go where?' He set his glass down, pulled the pipe from his mouth and leaned farther forward, clasping his hands before him. 'Let's get down to cases, lassie. The thing's simple enough. You be good to *me*, I'll be good to you.'

'For as long as it suits you,' she said. 'No, Red-Whiskers. I have pride, even if you do not.'

'Ye have a high opinion of yoursen, that's sure enough. But I'll wager ye'll see things a mite differently after ye've had the vinegar knocked out of ye.'

He lurched forward and made a grab for her. She leapt up, her own chair crashing over behind her. But before she could evade him altogether his stubby fingers closed on the front of her dress and tore the stitching along one shoulder-seam. The sight of her golden flesh excited him still further, and he quickly put his other hand on her and pushed her backward until she slammed hard against the wall.

For a split second then she was back at the creek, and Quintero was trying to fight her into submission by half-drowning her. She wondered fleetingly if the Indian agent was right; that this was all her life would ever consist of, unless she learned to accept the inevitable.

Todd pushed his face against hers, determined to steal a kiss. She turned her head away, but there was no escaping the unwashed smell of the man. As she struggled against him she thought of *Scan-To*; Sky-Eyes; Jesse. He had come to her aid once. It was too much to hope that he could help her again. She was alone now, and so. . . .

And so she did the only thing she could.

She brought her knee up hard between Calum Todd's legs.

Todd's groan escaped with a rush of sour air and he stumbled backward, doubled over his knees, cursing. She bolted for the door, tripped on a box and went sprawling. When she turned again he'd straightened back up, his face like chalk against the fiery scarlet of his beard. He glared at her. Then his lips peeled back to reveal his small teeth, and his hands folded into fists.

'Ye bitch,' he whispered. And then, in a furious bellow: '*Ye ungrateful little bitch!*'

As he came at her she made another try for the door. Long before she got there she felt his hand grasp her shoulder, spin her around. A second later his fist clubbed her along the side of her head and she stumbled sideways, dazed but still conscious. She staggered out of his reach but he came at her again, teeth clenched, brows lowered, a terrible promise of pain in his eyes.

There was no escape in the cramped room. Again he threw himself at her. She dodged aside and he blundered into the shelves there, making their burden of pots and pans tinkle discordantly.

Spinning around again he breathed: 'Och, ye'll pay now, lassie.'

He rushed at her again.

Eyes wide, she backed away, came up hard against the table. The legs shuddered across the floor, and as she moved sideways to put it between her and her attacker she saw the bottle he'd been drinking from and snatched it up.

As soon as he was within range she swung it around in a tight arc and. . . .

The thick, smeared bottle smashed against Calum Todd's left ear and whiskey splattered across his face, beard and one side of his food-stained half-placket shirt. The force of the blow slammed him sideways and, as she watched, his eyes rolled back in his head and he collapsed to the floor.

Morning Star swayed. She didn't even realize she'd released her grip on the jagged neck of the bottle until it shattered on the boards at her feet.

She stepped forward and peered down at the Indian agent.

She couldn't see him breathing.

As she looked, blood started to trickle from the gash in his scalp and puddle in his cut ear.

She fetched the lamp, took a closer look. There was no rise and fall to his chest.

Again she swayed. *I have killed him*, she thought.

And in that instant she knew she must leave this wretched place before the crime was discovered.

CHAPTER TEN

Jesse quit Fort Bowie at first light the following morning, trailing his supply-laden pack-mule behind him. Soon he was crossing vast barren flatlands broken every few miles by low gray hills. Grass was sparse, but there was no shortage of sagebrush.

He stopped sometime around noon to give himself and his animals a blow. He drank sparingly from his canteen, then spilled water into his upturned hat so that the horse and mule could drink as well. The day was oven-hot and shade on the sun-baked scrubland was non-existent. He felt gritty, sweaty and uncomfortable, and yet his thoughts were dominated not by Cochise or Geronimo or the impossible task he'd been given by President Grant, but by the girl he'd left behind – the girl, Morning Star.

He remounted and pushed on. The long afternoon wound inexorably toward dusk. At last the worst of the heat began to soak into the ground, and a new thought started nagging at him.

He drew rein and twisted around to check his back-trail. The rutted plain looked empty and lifeless. And yet he had the damnedest notion that he was anything but alone out here. It was nothing he could put his finger on, just a feeling . . . one he'd learned to trust a long time ago.

It was heading toward sunset; time to find a decent campsite while there was still light enough for the task. He spotted a nest of layered red rocks about a mile off the trail and pointed the sorrel toward it. There he saw to the animals, scooped a hollow in which he could build a fire that wouldn't be seen from level ground and boiled coffee and beans.

The feeling that he was being watched persisted. He got up and moved around a little, using the opportunity to scan his surroundings. He couldn't see anything out of the ordinary, but what did that prove? Damn all. Keeping his movements casual, he thumbed the restraining thong off the hammer of his holstered Colt and sat with his back propped against his upturned saddle, within easy reach of his carbine.

The sky turned from cerulean blue to cobalt, and then from cobalt to a star-studded ultramarine. As darkness overtook the land he forced himself to eat but was too tense to really taste the food. After the meal was finished he sat back again and pretended to doze. The Apaches were a brave people, but they had nothing against doing things the easy way. And though they hated to fight in the dark for fear that their spirits might get lost if they died in combat, there was little that was easier than taking a white man while he slept.

Out in the darkness he heard the softest rustle of sound. He forced himself to stay absolutely still, except for the slow rise and fall of his chest and the occasional fake snore for good measure.

There – again!

The head-shake of an impatient horse.

Someone was definitely out there.

The next sound he heard confirmed it. It was only the softest scuff, but enough to make him act. He sat up, turned toward the sound and even as he did so his hand came up heavy with Colt. He saw a silhouette, black against the blacker night, and was a fraction away from pulling the trigger when his so-called attacker said: 'Wait! Do not shoot, *Scan-To*! It is me!'

He'd been ready for a fight, prepared to kill rather than be killed, and it was an instant before he recognized her voice and was able to let the tension go. Realizing then that she had been the cause of his unease all along, Jesse got to his feet, and lowering the hammer on his Colt, said angrily: 'Morning Star? *Dammit*, girl, I might've known!'

She came closer while he spoke, leading her horse – a wiry little buckskin – until at last the light from the low fire showed him her large eyes, her slightly parted lips.

He wanted to swear, but instead just shook his head and holstered his gun.

'What in damnation are you doin' here?' he demanded. Then, as a new thought struck him: 'Where'd you get that horse, anyway? Don't tell me you stole it?'

She looked at him for a long moment before saying: 'I am not going back.'

'No, an' I can't force you to,' he said. 'But I'll tell you this much. You're not goin' on with me, an' that's the end of *that* rope.'

'I killed a man,' she said quietly.

He stared at her. Words deserted him for a few moments before he finally managed: 'You *what?*'

'The Indian agent,' she said. 'Todd.'

'What happened?'

'What do you *think* happened?'

'I don't want to guess. Tell me.'

'He was just like the *comancheros*. He thought I could be taken, used. He was wrong.'

'So you killed him?'

'I did not mean to.'

'That won't change anything.'

'This I know.'

'Shoot him?'

'I struck him with a whiskey bottle. Left him there, stole a horse from the stable and fled when it was dark.'

'An' came right after *me*,' he said, running his fingers through his shaggy hair.

'Who else was I to come after?'

He walked in a tight, frustrated circle. 'Yesterday you said you didn't need anyone!'

'Yesterday I had not killed a man.'

'Goddammit,' he said. He had enough on his plate as it was, without getting involved in murder as well – and that was exactly how a sonofabitch like Major Calloway would see it. The murder of an Indian agent, a government official . . . Christ, she'd be lucky if they didn't send a federal marshal after her.

'I am sorry,' she said wretchedly. 'I did not know who else to turn to.'

He studied her. Her eyes dropped from his. He wondered if she was trying to make him feel guilty. Well, she could try all she liked. It wasn't going to work. Then he remembered something.

'Earlier,' he said. 'Before you entered the camp – what did you call me?'

'I do not remember.'

He didn't believe her. But right then he had more important things to occupy his mind, and his word to keep to the President.

Again she said, 'I am sorry. I will go now.' Turning, she started to lead her stolen horse off into the ever-cooling night.

He watched her go. She was waiting for him to take pity on her and tell her to come back. He *knew* she was. But he wasn't going to. *Oh* no. She could ride north, south, east or west as far as he was concerned. But if she came with him she'd only be going one place – Cochise's mountain stronghold – and there was no telling just how *that* was going to pan out.

His pa had always urged him to live a careful life. 'Caution's the way, son,' he'd said. And his father had been a wise man. But now, as Jesse watched Morning Star slowly being swallowed up by the darkness, he thought: *For a man who thinks caution's the way, you're sure throwing caution to the wind tonight.*

'Morning Star!' he called. 'Come on back!'

She turned and stared at him, now barely visible in the darkness.

'Well? What you waitin' for?'

Still she stood there, unmoving.

'Don't you understand me, girl? I'm sayin' it's OK. You can come back. We'll find a way to sort this out. Got my word on it.'

Still no reaction.

'Dammit,' he exclaimed. 'Don't you get it? I ain't sore at you no more.'

'Then ask me,' she said finally.

'What?'

'*Ask* me to come back,' she said. 'Do not *tell* me.'

He gaped. 'You want me to *ask* you?'

She nodded.

'Jesus,' he grumbled. 'You don't want much, do you?'

She said nothing.

'OK,' he said at last. 'I'm askin' you. Come back.'

'Ask nicely. It is the only way I will do as you wish.'

'As I *wish*?' His voice rose with frustration. 'Hell's fire, girl. You got it kind of turned around, ain't you? I mean, you dog my trail without me knowin', you come bustin' into my camp askin' to be shot, and now you want me to beg you stay?'

'Not beg. Ask. As you would any white girl you respected.'

So there it was. When you boiled it down it was strictly a matter of pride, he realized. Pride and . . . respect.

He chewed on his cheek for a moment. What was that saying, about folks who could try the patience of saints?

Jesus.

Eventually, he said: '*Please will you stay*? Is that good enough?'

He glimpsed her smile through the gloom and when she started back toward the camp, he figured it was.

'Women,' he muttered. 'Sometimes I think a man could get along better with a two-legged, blind mule!'

CHAPTER ELEVEN

The Apache lookout saw them coming when they were still a long ways off. There were two of them, a man and a woman both walking their horses across the vast, scorched sagebrush plain below, the girl holding the reins to the pack-mule trailing behind them. The lookout frowned curiously, for the girl was undoubtedly Apache. What, then, was she doing with one of the hated *wasichu*?

They came a quarter-mile closer before the lookout received an answer of sorts. The White-Eyes stopped and reached for something attached to his saddle. The lookout stiffened when he saw the man draw a carbine from its sheath. But a moment later the man produced a white kerchief from his jacket and tied it to the barrel. Holding the makeshift flag of truce high, he mounted up, the girl followed suit, and they started riding slowly toward him again.

Carefully, the lookout checked the seemingly endless desert flatlands below in case these two were but a diversion. But there was no one else down there, he was certain of it.

At last he turned, drew an arrow from the fringed lion-

63

skin quiver at his back and shot the missile toward the southeast. It arced into the nude blue sky and finally landed in an area of Cochise's stronghold where their ponies often grazed. There another lookout snatched it from the ground and held it high so the archer could see that his warning had been received. Then, breaking into a run, this lookout took the arrow to Cochise, who would decide the fate of the newcomers.

Jesse's belly had clenched tight when he first saw the mountains rising up from out of rocky foothills in a series of seamed turrets and granite domes. Nothing could have prepared him for their size. They stretched from one end of the horizon to the other, and from this point they seemed to tilt toward the southeast like a series of gigantic, storm-tossed waves frozen in time.

Cochise had certainly chosen his stronghold well. No one was ever going to take him by surprise as long as he remained holed-up there. Those almost unreachable battlements were protected by near-vertical slopes that no army could ever hope to storm or scale.

Jesse felt Morning Star's eyes on him and looked back at her. It had taken them three days to reach this place; three days in which he had fallen in love with her.

'It is not too late to turn back,' she said.

'It is for me.'

She smiled. 'It is the answer I expected.'

'Then quit testin' me.'

'Perhaps I am testing myself.'

He hadn't thought of that. 'You're a strange one, you know that?'

'I am an Apache,' she said simply. 'You are white.

Everything between us is strange.'

'I know,' he said, wryly. 'I'm workin' on that.'

They pushed on. The mountains dwarfed them, dwarfed everything . . . even the small group of riders who appeared around a low, conical foothill twenty minutes later, and came straight on at a gallop.

Jesse reined up and held the makeshift flag of truce high.

'You do not seem surprised that they have come to meet us,' said Morning Star, also bringing her mount to a halt.

'Actually, I was countin' on it. Figured we'd never find Cochise up there otherwise.'

'You are wise.'

'For a white man?'

'For *any* man.'

Facing front again Jesse counted an even dozen Apaches, then corrected himself: eleven Apaches and a single black man who rode with them. His throat dried a little and he licked his lips, realizing suddenly that he was out of spit.

'This is it, Morning Star,' he warned. 'If we can't get past this bunch, we're cooked – and I'm real sorry I brought you out here.'

'Perhaps such a fate is all I deserve.'

'For killing that Indian agent? I doubt it. Truth is, you might just have done the world a favor there.'

The Apaches were close enough now for Jesse to make out individual details – the yellow headband on one, the square of buckskin that served as another's saddle. They were all armed, all wearing the white slash of paint across their cheeks and noses that denoted war.

When they were within arrow-shot they slowed, fanned

out into a line, and gradually the line closed at both ends around them, like pincers. Horses blew, shook their heads and stamped their feet. Jesse looked from one brave to another, somehow finding the strength to keep the uneasiness off his face and show them only a confidence he didn't really feel.

His gaze finally locked on the amber eyes of the black man. He felt – hoped – he might have an ally in this man, though he had no idea why.

Presently, their leader spoke in fluent Spanish.

Jesse raised his hand, stopping him. '*Solo se un poco de español,*' he said. Then, as the Apache stared impassively at him: 'Do you speak English?'

'I can translate for you,' Morning Star began; then broke off as the leader shouted angrily at her in Apache.

'I have offended him by daring to speak,' she whispered to Jesse.

'*Hablas Ingles?*' he asked the leader.

Contempt narrowed the Apache's dark brown eyes. 'This is Apache land,' he said in guttural English. 'All others who cross it must die.'

Jesse sat straighter in the saddle and squared his shoulders. 'It is as I have heard, then. The Apaches are gutless dogs without respect.'

There was a shocked intake of breath, not least from Morning Star.

'You will not talk so bravely when hot coals fill your mouth!' promised the leader.

Jesse eyed him levelly. 'Among men of honor, the flag I hold protects those who come to talk.'

'Then talk,' said the Apache. 'I, Geronimo, will listen. But then I will kill you.'

Jesse thought sourly: *Thank you, Mr President. That's the last time I vote for you damn Republicans.*

Then Morning Star said softly: 'You have not changed, Goyahkla. Anger still rules your wisdom.'

Geronimo looked at her, surprise showing briefly on his usually inscrutable face. 'Who calls me by my tribal name?'

'It is I, Morning Star, daughter of Pale Dawn and Man-Who-Paints-The-Sky.'

Geronimo leaned forward and studied her, trying to place her. The sudden, imperceptible relaxing of his expression told them that finally he remembered her. 'You have grown from a straggly weed to a blooming flower,' he said, almost grudgingly. 'But that will not save the white man's life.'

Beside him Zulu Sam shifted a little, the movement catching Geronimo's eye as he'd intended it to.

Geronimo looked challengingly at the Zulu. 'You would have a say in this, Haskiiyii-Thii?'

Sam said diplomatically: 'If Geronimo wants to prove that he's worthy of ruling the Chiricahuas, let him start now.'

'How?'

'When I was small, a spider bit me. From then on I killed all spiders, until one day my father taught me that some spiders can be trusted *not* to bite.'

'This man is not a spider,' Geronimo said obstinately. 'He is a White-Eyes, and *all* White-Eyes bite.'

'Maybe. But a wise chief would take this man to the elders, so they may hear his words at the Council fire before deciding whether he lives or dies.'

Geronimo considered that. Reluctantly he had to admit that *Haskiiyii-Thii* was right. Just as there was a time for

67

action, so too was there a time for restraint. Continuing to glower at Jesse, he nodded in agreement. 'Take their weapons,' he ordered at last, 'and bring them along.'

He whirled his pony about and rode back toward the conical foothill.

As the other Apaches crowded around Jesse and Morning Star, Sam eased in between them and took Jesse's Colt and Winchester.

Jesse looked gratefully at him. 'Thanks.'

Sam stuffed the Colt into his waistband, then rested the Winchester across his lap. 'Save your thanks till whatever it is you want pans out the right way,' he said.

CHAPTER TWELVE

The Apaches herded their prisoners ever deeper into the mountains. Around them, huge boulders balanced precariously on steep hillsides, while marginally smaller rocks, twisted over the ages into all manner of bizarre shapes, gave the terrain an unsettling, dreamlike quality. After a time the steep rocky trail yielded to grassy meadows studded with enormous oaks; here Jesse spotted the tracks of mountain lion, deer and coyote.

About two hours later they passed the open shaft of a long-abandoned mine. As he walked his horse past it Jesse peered inside and saw that the shaft dropped at least thirty feet before twisting away to the left. He remembered what Patch had said about Grant working for the miners and wondered if he could have misread the President's intentions. Maybe this wasn't about peace at all. Maybe it really was about business, and the fortune in precious metals these hills were said to contain.

It was a troublesome thought.

The brush and small trees grew thicker. Jesse recognized juniper, fir, madrone and mountain oak. As the day wore on the steep rocky slopes became choked with agave, sotol and small, prickly cacti. Soon the mixture of scrub and trees grew so close together that they had to fight their way through the natural barrier.

Five hours into the trek Geronimo threw one last glance back at Morning Star – he'd been stealing glances at her all day, Jesse had noticed – then forged ahead without a word to anyone and was soon lost to sight. A short time later a series of gentle ridges led them toward a smooth crest, and Jesse wondered if this was the *Mount Glenn* that was marked on his map.

When they eventually topped out and saw Cochise's stronghold below them, he knew that it was.

He and the girl exchanged an uneasy look.

The long, wide canyon was a rugged natural fortress shaded by large oaks. A maze of small, hide-covered wickiups and round, earth-and-wood-built lodges surrounded the spacious central area. Jesse tried to estimate their number but quickly gave up. There were just too many. He saw a pool surrounded by yucca and rocks, its water showing black and oily from this elevation. And as they descended toward the camp, he thought he heard the rush of a waterfall somewhere beyond the trees.

A stream ran through the village, effectively slicing it in two. Here women washed clothes while their babies splashed and giggled, and horses stood hock-deep, drinking their fill. More horses grazed on the lush grass that grew just about everywhere.

As Sam led them into the village a pack of gaunt, yapping dogs hurtled out of nowhere to greet them. Drawn by the commotion, curious adults and children came out and stared suspiciously at the white man. Again, it was impossible to calculate their numbers. There were hundreds of them, the majority women in colorful blouses and skirts, many carrying baskets or cradleboards.

That wasn't to say there was any shortage of men. There wasn't. Truth be told, there were a damn sight more braves around than Jesse cared to see right then – and none of them looked especially friendly.

Geronimo, he saw, had dismounted outside one of the larger lodges fringing the central area. He stood next to a taller, older Apache whose black, gray-tinged hair spilled to his broad shoulders. Geronimo pointed them out as they came closer.

Jesse focused on Geronimo's companion, and felt a new knot of tension grab his stomach.

If this was Cochise, as he suspected, then the Apache had been well named. In Chiricahua, Cochise translated as 'oak', and the man who now commanded his attention looked as if he'd been carved from it. In a sun-faded blue shirt with a red breechclout cloth hanging over his white cotton pants, wide, conch-decorated belt and knee-high moccasins, he was the very image of strength and dignity. He had well-spaced brown eyes, a prominent Roman nose, hollow cheeks and a wide mouth turned down at the corners. He was well into his fifties, but far from diminishing him, his years gave him a quiet authority.

Sam brought his mount to a halt before the lodge and the others did likewise. A heavy, expectant silence settled over the stronghold. Even the dogs stopped yapping. At last the man beside Geronimo said: 'I am Cochise. Why do you come here, White-Eyes?'

Jesse took a deep breath and said: 'I bring words of peace from the Great White Chief in Washington.'

Cochise only curled his lip. 'I have heard these words

71

before. Yet still my people die from your soldiers' bullets.'

'This I know,' Jesse said solemnly. 'But it doesn't have to be that way, Cochise. I carry papers giving me permission to speak for the Great White Chief, and he wants only peace.'

'Words. . . . The Apaches are tired of talk that always ends in betrayal. So go back to where you came from, White-Eyes, and be grateful that Cochise honors your pale flag.'

He was about to re-enter his lodge when Jesse took a chance and said desperately: 'Wait!'

The chief turned back, his expression asking the question.

Jesse reached into his shirt and Geronimo instinctively took a pace forward in case he was reaching for a hidden weapon. But all Jesse brought out was a talisman he'd always worn around his neck. It was a withered eagle's talon painted yellow and blue, bound tightly together with dried grass and feathers.

'I bring you this,' Jesse said, holding it up.

Frowning, Cochise came forward, reached up and took the talisman between his fingers. 'This is strong medicine, White-Eyes. Where did you get it?'

'From Sitting Bull, of the Sioux nation.'

'I have heard the name,' allowed Cochise. 'Sitting Bull gave you this?'

'Yes.'

'Sitting Bull *himself*?'

'Yes.'

'Why did he do this thing?'

'My pa was an Indian agent for the Sioux. He was a good man, and the Sioux knew it. He got to be friends

72

with most of the chiefs, like Red Cloud and Sitting Bull. I guess Sitting Bull took a shine to me, as well.'

The Chiricahua searched Jesse's face for any evidence of deception. Finding none, he reached a decision within himself and said: 'Come.'

Behind him Geronimo made a sound of disgust. 'Pah! You swallow these lies?'

Cochise said simply: 'They are *not* lies.'

'The White-Eyes *always* lie!'

'In this man's eyes I see only the truth, Goyahkla.'

Geronimo was about to say more but suddenly changed his mind, turned on his heel and stormed off.

Jesse exchanged another glance with Morning Star. Then both dismounted and followed Cochise into his lodge. It was dark and dusty inside, even though the buffalo-hide sides had been rolled back to let in a cooling breeze.

'Wait here while I talk to the elders and ask them to hear your words,' Cochise told him.

'Will I be alive when you return?' Jesse said.

Cochise looked disdainful, almost offended. 'You will be safe, White-Eyes. No one will dare harm you.'

'*Ashoge*,' Jesse said politely. It was an expression of gratitude that Morning Star had taught him.

Cochise studied him a moment longer, then said: '*A he ya eh*. But I promise nothing.'

'I don't expect you to.'

'This I will say, though. Do not let Geronimo's anger distress you. He is young and still has much to learn about the ways of peace.'

'Don't we all?'

'Still, he is a true warrior. And my people need him and

73

others like him, if we are to survive against your soldiers.'

Jesse nodded, then indicated Morning Star. 'About the girl,' he said. 'She lost her family in a *comanchero* raid almost a week ago. She needs shelter.'

Cochise eyed her thoughtfully. 'She will find it here,' he said at length. Then, to Morning Star: 'Come with me.'

Morning Star gave Jesse one last look, then followed Cochise outside.

Jesse was left alone.

CHAPTER THIRTEEN

Wordlessly Cochise strode through the village until he came to a thin path that led to higher ground. Feisty as she was, Morning Star followed obediently in his wake. Being in the presence of her own people again had made her feel happy and sad at the same time – happy because the familiar sights, sounds and smells reminded her of the life she had known before the comancheros had come, and sad that it had all had to end so abruptly.

The trail eventually opened out and led through timber to a clearing at the center of which a lone woman stood with head bent before a large cairn of stones. Morning Star hesitated momentarily, for this was clearly a burial ceremony, and as such was a private affair at which she had no business.

When a warrior dies, there is a great public outpouring of grief. When a squaw dies, it is usually a matter of little consequence that, more often than not, goes unnoticed by all but her closest friends and female relatives. It is the Apache way. In private, the bereaved – male *and* female – may express their grief freely, but never, ever in public.

Cochise knew this, and yet still he had brought her to

this spot, where this woman was mourning the passing of one of her own.

Hearing their arrival, the woman turned and quickly composed herself. She was in her forties, her glossy black hair tied back with a length of yellow yarn. She wore a short, beaded cape over a plain green dress, and the pain of her loss was clear to see on her lined round face. The tears that had so reddened her eyes still shone on her cheeks.

'Nervous Woman,' Cochise said respectfully. 'Forgive this intrusion upon your grief.'

Nervous Woman inclined her head. 'It is generous of Cochise to share his heart with mine.'

In a gesture that was typical Apache, Cochise indicated the cairn with a thrust of his chin. 'Your daughter was a fine woman,' he said, observing his people's custom of not using the dead girl's name. 'She did not deserve the Sickness-That-Wastes. But just as there is a sunrise after every sunset, so too there can be happiness after pain.'

Nervous Woman nodded, but without any real conviction.

'This girl,' Cochise continued, 'is called Morning Star. She has recently lost loved ones of her own. It is therefore my wish that you welcome her into the lodge you share with Bear's Paw . . . and once more become a family.'

The squaw looked at Morning Star as if noticing her for the first time. Morning Star looked back at her, showing no emotion but finding it easy to identify with her pain. Fresh tears again welled in Nervous Woman's eyes. But she stepped forward and folded her arms gently around Morning Star. Morning Star stiffened and at first made no response. Then Nervous Woman sobbed – a small, muffled sound that carried all the hurt of the world in it – and all at once Morning Star melted against the older squaw and with tears spilling down her own cheeks, hugged Nervous Woman back with all her heart.

Cochise nodded with approval. 'It is good,' he said.

And so it was.

The long, hot afternoon dragged on. With no choice in the matter, Jesse stayed inside the lodge and listened to camp-life going on around him. Women busied themselves with domestic chores or sat their children down and patiently taught them the skills they would need in later life. The children – by nature well-behaved and obedient – were keen and happy to learn. Once he was woken from a light doze by the sound of a small group singing. It wasn't unusual for groups of any size to sing and pray to their gods, and he found it curiously soothing.

Toward dusk a small band of hunters rode in, their bodies still glistening with the animal fat they'd used to disguise their scent. Going to the lodge entrance, Jesse saw that they had brought down several deer and antelope, even an elk.

Well beyond Jesse's range of vision, Geronimo watched Zulu Sam talking with Morning Star outside her new home. He felt a sharp twinge of jealousy, for she had indeed grown into a beautiful woman. As he turned away he saw his friends, Blue Crow, Runs Slowly and Little Wolf, watching him with amusement, and scowled. Blue Crow jokingly tried to kiss Little Wolf, and they all started laughing. Irked, Geronimo snatched up a rock and threw it at them. The young braves scattered, laughing even harder.

Cochise, meanwhile, sat among a circle of Apache elders in the Council lodge on the other side of the camp and explained all about the white man who had come to talk peace with them. They were as dismissive as he had been at first, until he told them that this man carried with him strong medicine from none other than Sitting Bull. Then the elders looked at each other, impressed, and continued passing a pipe with a long redwood stem between them.

With nothing else to occupy him, Jesse finally stretched out, tipped his hat over his eyes and made another stab at sleeping. Cochise had said he would be safe here, and he had no reason to doubt him. But sleep remained elusive, and when he heard a small sound in the lodge doorway some time later he sat up with a start.

Morning Star stood in the entrance, a pitcher of water in one hand and a bowl of steaming acorn stew in the other.

As she came inside and set the meal down, he got to his feet. 'Are you OK?' he asked, glad to see her again.

'Of course.'

'Have they set you up all right? You know, found you someplace to live?'

'I have a new family. I am now the daughter of Nervous Woman and Bear's Paw. They are good people.'

'I'm glad.' He looked at her for a moment longer, then said: 'Has there been any word from Cochise yet?'

'It is not for me to speak the words of my chief,' she replied, and turned back toward the door. There, she

78

paused briefly, looked at him once more and added softly: 'No word yet.'

Jesse continued to wait.

CHAPTER FOURTEEN

Sometime around the middle of the following morning the lodge doorway suddenly darkened and Geronimo snapped: 'Come.'

By now heartily sick of being cooped up, Jesse grabbed his hat and followed him outside, squinting in the harsh glare of the new day. Though he was still a novelty to the Apaches whom he passed, their stares were no longer filled with hostility.

Geronimo led him briskly through the stronghold until they reached the Council lodge, a large oval structure constructed from bent, brush-covered saplings. Without pause he led Jesse inside.

The lodge was dark and ill-lit. Cochise and a group of eight elderly Apaches sat cross-legged around the room's shadowy edges, many smoking pipes. The air was thick with the smell of sumac leaves and tree bark, willow, bearberry and sage, and it was all Jesse could do not to cough.

When Cochise indicated that Jesse should sit cross-legged facing them, he did so immediately. Wanting to get

things off to a good start, he carefully signed his thanks to
the elders for agreeing to listen to him. These hand gestures were something else Morning Star had taught him.

The elders did not look impressed.

Not one of them was less than eighty. They were small,
frail, thin-faced men, many of them toothless, with gray
brittle hair and sunken eyes. Once they had been as for-
midable in appearance as Cochise and Geronimo were
now, and in a way they still were, for they were that tough-
est of breeds – *survivors* – and their wisdom was held in
high esteem by those they counseled.

One of them finally said something in Apache and
Cochise translated for him. 'Nantan says you may speak
your piece.'

'My Apache is poor, Cochise. Will they understand what
I say in English?'

'I will translate for those who don't. Now, speak.'

Jesse nodded his thanks and looked at the elders. 'The
Great White Chief in Washington wants the Apaches to
live in peace with their white brothers,' he began.

'Yes – but where?' countered a wrinkled Apache at the
far end of the line, whose left eye was filmed over. His
voice was a high croak, his English broken but good. 'On
useless land governed by men who would cheat them?'

'It's true that the Great White Chief *does* want you to live
on a reservation,' Jesse admitted. 'But he has given me his
word that the land will be fertile and that he'll appoint an
honest Indian agent who'll treat the Apaches fairly.'

'As the man at Fort Bowie does?' asked another.

He was referring to Calum Todd – the man Morning
Star had killed.

'I know little about that man,' Jesse replied. 'But I

promise you this. The Apaches will be shown the respect and dignity that is their due. You have my word on it.'

'The word of a white man is as useless as hairs on a snake,' snorted Geronimo, from the doorway.

'Sometimes this is true,' Jesse admitted. 'But this is also true: not all white men are liars, any more than all Apaches are murderers.'

He looked around as he spoke and saw the elders nodding in agreement.

'Anyway, what have you got to lose by making peace?'

'Our freedom,' another elder grunted immediately. His companions muttered their agreement.

'Peace is one thing, White-Eyes, it is a *good* thing,' said Cochise. 'But why should we have to live where the white man tells us, so that we may achieve it?'

'The white man feels a responsibility toward you,' Jesse replied. 'To look after you.'

'Are we children who cannot look after themselves?'

'Of course not. But the white man has *knowledge* about civilization that you do not, Cochise. You can learn from him.'

'Learn how to plow the earth and live on Indian corn?' asked the Apache with the milky eye. 'These things we know already.'

'There are other things. *Important* things. Medicine to cure sickness, schools to teach your young ones how to read and write, machinery to make life easier for everyone. These things are normal in a civilized world, as you will learn—'

Cochise cut him off. 'No, White-Eyes. We will learn only what your people *want* us to learn, and no more.'

'Why do you say that?'

82

'Because this is the only way you will have control over us. And control is what you want. Live here, eat this, not that, pray to our gods, not yours, do what we tell you – it is all a matter of control, of keeping us under your thumb. And Apaches cannot live this way. They *will* not live this way.'

Jesse started to say something but Cochise raised his hand, silencing him. 'So tell your Great White Chief this,' he continued. 'The Apaches do not want war. We have lost too many of our young men already. But war is better than living like cattle behind fences, or being treated as children. We Apaches were born free and we will live free. And if Ussen, the Creator, wills it, we will die free – on our own land.'

Jesse sagged. 'You will not agree to the Great White Chief's terms, then?'

'We will make peace,' said Cochise, 'but we will not live on a reservation, like dogs under the white man's eye.'

Jesse drew a breath. 'Well, it's not the answer the Great White Chief wants to hear, but I'll pass it along. And maybe when he weighs the alternatives, he'll see reason. But you'll have to give me some kind of proof that will assure him the Apaches can live in peace with the white man.'

Two of the elders did not understand everything Jesse had said. Cochise translated for them. A brief but heated debate followed.

Cochise then told Jesse: 'We will give you an answer when the morning sun again yawns in the sky. Meanwhile, you are free to roam the stronghold.'

Jesse nodded his thanks. '*Ashoge*,' he said again.

CHAPTER FIFTEEN

Glad of the chance to stretch his legs, Jesse left the lodge and went in search of Morning Star. As he walked through the stronghold, past warriors, women and children, he realized they were no longer curious about him; he had been accepted by their chief and that was enough for them.

Although Jesse didn't see Geronimo, he could feel the Apache's angry eyes on his back every step of the way. He chose not to pause or look around, knowing this would send a message to anyone watching that he felt fear.

Presently, he spotted the girl kneeling beside the stream, spreading freshly washed clothes on a rock to dry. When she saw him watching her she got to her feet and smiled at him.

'You have spoken with the elders?' she asked.

'Uh-huh.'

'But it did not go the way you hoped?'

'That obvious, huh?' He looked around. 'Walk with me?'

'I have work to do.'

'This might be the last time I see you,' he said regretfully. 'Reckon I'll be leavin' tomorrow.'

Morning Star considered a moment, then said: 'If we walk among the trees, no one will see us and tell my new family that I am not working.'

As they headed for some nearby oaks, he said: 'How do you like them, anyway? Are they treating you well?'

'Yes. Bear's Paw likes my cooking and Nervous Woman does not beat me too hard.'

'Sounds like you struck gold,' he said drily.

'It has been a time of sadness for all of us,' she said. 'But now comes a time of renewal.' Her hazel eyes searched his face. 'Is this really the last time I will see you?'

'Would it matter to you if it was?'

It was on the tip of her tongue to say that it would, very much. But then she realized he was fishing and said instead: 'Not at all. Already I have many new friends, and Nervous Woman keeps me busy. I shall probably not even notice when you are gone.'

Hiding his smile he said: 'That's good to know. See, if I *did* come back, I was plannin' on buyin' you a gift. Now, I'll spend the money on one of the pretty women at the fort instead.'

She did not respond. Nor could he tell by her expression what she was thinking. After a little she said carefully: 'This gift you were thinking of buying me? Would I have liked it?'

'Guess we'll never know, will we?' He stopped then, faced her and impulsively pulled her close. 'Unless, of course, you change your mind about missin'—'

There was a sudden crackling of brush behind them, followed by a loud, angry bellow. Even as Jesse turned, a massive black bear charged out of the trees and reared up on its hind legs.

Instinctively he reached for his Colt, realized it wasn't there and yelled: 'Get behind me!'

But to his surprise, the girl pushed him aside and snapped: 'Wait! He will not hurt you!'

As the bear growled again Jesse said: 'Tell *him* that!'

The creature stood almost as tall as Jesse and weighed at least 300 pounds. Its sloping shoulders were broad and muscular, its claws short but deadly. It glared down at Jesse through tiny, close-set eyes. There was a distinctive white crescent-moon shape in the fur of its chest.

'He is friendly,' Morning Star said quickly. 'He just thought you were hurting me.' And to the bear: 'It is all right, Little One.'

Jesse's eyebrows arched. *Little One?*

'It is a word of endearment more than size.'

He watched as she faced the bear, extended her hands toward it and started crooning softly, making sounds Jesse had never heard before. To his amazement the bear dropped slowly to all fours and then approached her.

Jesse thought: *Just grab her and run. Run and pray you can out-distance that sonofa—*

The bear lumbered up to Morning Star and rubbed his head against one of her outstretched hands. Jesse swallowed, told himself he couldn't possibly be seeing what he *thought* he was seeing.

He realized then that the bear had turned its beady eyes back on him, its expression one of withering disdain. It offered him one final warning growl, then turned around and plodded back into the trees.

Feeling shaky, Jesse released a pent-up breath. 'Next time you think we might run into one of your, uh, "friends",' he said thickly, 'tell me ahead of time, OK?'

She cocked her head at him. 'Did he *scare* you?'

'Curled my toes,' he confessed. 'Who taught you all that croonin' stuff, anyway?'

'*Haskiiyii-Thii*,' she said, and when the question showed on his face: 'The man with skin like darkness, whom some call Zulu Sam. Yesterday he and I walked this very path, and Little One appeared. *Haskiiyii-Thii* did as you saw just now, and Little One calmed and went on his way.'

'And this Sam feller, he taught you how to do it?' Jesse said, trying not to acknowledge the irrational stab of jealousy that went through him.

She nodded.

'A man could turn gray overnight, steppin' out with you,' he said. Then: 'Come on, let's—'

'*White-Eyes!*'

Jesse turned with a start and saw that Geronimo was watching them from the trail. The Apache had been as noiseless as a shadow.

'This woman is Chiricahua now,' Geronimo said sternly, coming closer. 'You will leave her alone.'

Jesse wanted to tell him to go to hell. But he quickly reminded himself that he was here to make peace. Though it galled him to back down, he nodded and said: 'I'm not doin' her any harm. But neither do I want to offend your people.'

'Then go,' said Geronimo. '*Now.* I would talk with her alone.'

Jesse realized then that Geronimo was deliberately trying to provoke him. Maybe he was just showing off in front of Morning Star. Maybe he wanted to discredit Jesse in front of Cochise. Or perhaps he was just plain spoiling for a fight.

Well, Jesse wasn't going to accommodate him. He looked at Morning Star, saw the concern on her face and forced a smile to show that everything was all right and that there wasn't going to be any trouble.

But as he started back the way he'd come he heard Geronimo mutter something ugly and immediately swung back.

'What did you say?'

Geronimo's smile was wolfish. 'I said *coward*,' he replied, relishing the word. 'Like all white men, you are just a coward.'

Jesse stared him and thought: *Don't let him rile you*. And somehow he forced himself to say in a low grim voice: 'I reckon you're welcome to your opinion.'

Geronimo's grin actually widened. 'Then be on your way . . . *coward*.'

Jesse swallowed, nodded and tried to do just that. But somehow he just couldn't get his legs to cooperate. Instead he stayed right where he was for several seconds – and then he punched Geronimo full in the face.

CHAPTER SIXTEEN

As the blow sent Geronimo stumbling backward, Morning Star screamed: 'Stop it! I don't want you fighting over me!'

But this wasn't about her. And even though Jesse knew he'd fallen right into Geronimo's trap he still went after the Apache, peace be damned. He threw another punch that grazed Geronimo's jaw, and again Geronimo fell back and shook his head to clear it.

Then he came at Jesse like a mountain lion, face twisted with rage, teeth clamped tight, long hair flying wildly. He smashed into Jesse and the pair of them went sprawling. They rolled over and over, grappling, punching each other. Then Jesse threw Geronimo off, and both men quickly leapt to their feet.

Breathing hard, they circled each other, each glaring into the other's eyes. Then Geronimo attacked, cat-quick, and struck Jesse alongside the jaw. Jesse staggered back, crashing through the trees and bushes, out in the open.

As he picked himself up, he heard Morning Star scream and realized that he'd inadvertently given his back to his opponent. He wheeled around, got a glimpse of Geronimo charging him, and then the Apache leapt up and drop-kicked him.

Pain speared through Jesse's ribs and the force of the blow knocked him back into the grass. Geronimo tried to jump on him and break his ribs, but this time Jesse rolled aside.

Still, there was no time to recover. As he tried to get up Geronimo came for him again, this time at a run. Again they collided and grappled. Jesse butted Geronimo in the face and the Apache grunted and stumbled away, bleeding from the nose.

Jesse heard himself yelling as if from a vast distance: '*That's it! That's it*! It's over!'

But Geronimo didn't hear him, or if he did he chose to ignore him. He came in slower this time, and as other Apaches came running to watch the fight, he suddenly closed the gap between them in a single lunge. He kicked at Jesse's right shin and Jesse went down. But before Geronimo could follow through Jesse grabbed a fistful of dust and threw it into his face. Geronimo reared back, temporarily blinded. Jesse tackled him, and momentum carried the pair of them off the bank and into the stream.

They landed in an explosion of water, momentarily went under and then surfaced again, punching each other all the while. Geronimo caught Jesse a devastating blow on the temple. Stunned, Jesse collapsed. Geronimo moved quickly to drown him, and the cold, round pebbles at the bottom of the stream pressed hard against Jesse's teeth and face.

Getting his hands underneath him he pushed upward and broke the surface with a water-logged roar. Geronimo flew back off his shoulders and vanished beneath the water. He reappeared almost immediately, gasping.

They were just about to clash again when Zulu Sam threw himself into the stream and put himself between them, holding his powerful arms wide to make sure they kept their distance from each other.

'That's enough!' he roared.

But it wasn't. Both men ignored him and went at each other again. Even though they were evenly matched, neither man would give in. His face an uncharacteristic mask of rage, Jesse went to swing at Geronimo but Sam beat him to it. He belted Jesse on the jaw and Jesse went down in crash of water.

Geronimo gave a tight-lipped smile and lunged forward to drown Jesse – but then Sam punched him, too.

The world was tilting madly around Jesse when he eventually pushed himself back to the surface, gasping for breath. At first he was only dimly aware of what had happened. He saw Sam staring down at him. Then he looked at Geronimo, who was on his knees a few yards away, blood smearing his face.

You're a fool, Jesse, he told himself. *The President sent you out here to talk about peace and all you've done is gone and started a whole new war instead.*

He saw Morning Star watching him from the bank, her expression hard to read. She looked concerned for him, and that was good. But she also looked disappointed in him, and that wasn't.

He grew aware that the gathered Apaches had suddenly parted, and turned his head a little as Cochise stormed up. The chief looked down at the three men in the stream and his mouth tightened dangerously.

'What happened here?' he demanded.

Jesse sucked down another breath. 'Little . . .

91

misunderstanding is . . . all,' he said.

But Cochise wasn't fooled. 'You have disgraced me!' he told Geronimo. 'This man was under my protection. Yet, knowing this, still you attacked him! You have dishonored me, Geronimo!'

'We've both . . . dishonored you,' Jesse said quickly. 'He was spoilin' for a fight, but I obliged him. I'd say we're guilty as each other, Cochise.'

While Cochise absorbed his words, Jesse stood in the sunshine, chest still heaving. A few feet away, Geronimo was his mirror image. At last Jesse recovered enough to step forward and offer his hand. Geronimo's lips curled and he ignored it.

Cochise said: 'You will take this man's hand, Goyahkla. You will take it, or you will leave the stronghold!'

Geronimo stared at him, eyes wide with disbelief. 'You would favor a white man over an Apache?'

'Cochise's word favors no man. Once it is given, it must be obeyed.'

Geronimo said nothing but inwardly he raged.

Jesse was just about to withdraw his hand when the Apache took it, albeit grudgingly. They shook, neither saying a word. Then Geronimo turned and angrily waded ashore.

CHAPTER SEVENTEEN

Jesse limped back to Cochise's lodge, favoring his aching chest and pounding head. There he stripped to the waist and checked his ribs. There was soreness and some bruising, but he didn't think anything was broken. He washed and carefully put his shirt back on, then gingerly stretched out and told himself again that he'd been a fool.

Once again he remembered what his father had always taught him: *Caution's the way, son.* Well, he sure as hell hadn't been cautious this time. He'd told Cochise that his father had been a good man, and so he was. He'd always tried to live by the Bible, and though he had no deep religious beliefs Jesse had always tried to do likewise. But somewhere along the line all that stuff about turning the other cheek must have passed him by.

For the rest of that day he expected and dreaded a visit from Cochise. The Apache would order him to take his horse and mule and leave; there would never be peace between them – he and Geronimo had proved that beyond all doubt.

But no such visit came. Along toward sundown,

however, Zulu Sam poked his head through the entrance and said: 'How you feelin', Glover?'

'Like a fool.'

'Well, don't fret about it – no one's ever died from it yet.' He smiled, revealing strong, startlingly white teeth, and added: 'Come on. Somethin' here I think you'll want to see.'

Puzzled, Jesse got stiffly to his feet. 'What is it?'

'That girl o' yours,' said Sam.

'What about her?'

'She's changin' her name. An' Cochise has invited you to witness the ceremony.'

Surprised, Jesse joined the Zulu outside and settled his hat gingerly atop his still-aching head. 'That mean I'm still in Cochise's good books?'

'Don't think you were ever in his bad ones. Geronimo's been spoilin' for a fight ever since you got here. Cochise knows that.'

'But I shouldn't have hit him. I had a great chance to prove that we could be better than that, and I didn't take it.'

Sam shrugged. 'Don't be so hard on yourself. If you'd backed down, you would've looked like a coward. Cochise knows *that*, too. Anyway, if it's any consolation, I think you did the right thing. Taking on one Apache in a whole damn' stronghold full of 'em? That took guts, Glover. And if there's one thing every Apache respects, it's courage. An' that goes double for Cochise.'

Hearing that made Jesse feel a little better.

'You ever witnessed one of these name-changin' cere-monies?' Sam asked as they walked through the fire-lit camp.

'Nope. Seen the Cheyenne dance for buffalo one time. Even been to a Sioux weddin' ceremony. But name-changin' . . . that's a new one on me. How about you?'

'Zulus don't change their names,' Sam replied. 'They just add new ones to their old ones.' He grinned as a thought hit him. 'I knew an old chief once. His name was so long that . . . well, let's just say a man could go hungry waitin' for him to spit out the whole thing.'

Jesse's laugh was cut short as they arrived at a cleared area to the west of the camp, where a fire burned brightly outside the wickiup Bear's Paw shared with Nervous Woman. Amber shadows striped the faces of the people who had gathered there. Sam led Jesse through the crowd until they reached Cochise and Geronimo. Geronimo glared at him. In the restless light he looked as battered as Jesse felt. Then Jesse felt Cochise's eyes on him, and moved stiffly when the chief signed that he should be seated.

'You move as if a buffalo trampled you, White-Eyes.'

'Ask Geronimo how *he* feels,' Jesse said.

Cochise hid a smile. 'It is time,' he said then. 'The girl you brought here – she ends one life this night and begins another. And since she owes you that life, it is only right that you should be here to see it.'

Just then the ceremonial drummers began to beat a slow, primal rhythm. A moment later Morning Star emerged from Bear's Paw's wickiup, followed by Bear's Paw himself, and Nervous Woman. Between them they removed a blanket from the girl's bare shoulders and with a sudden intake of breath Jesse realized that she was naked from the waist up. At once he knew a dizzy moment of unreality mixed with desire, for she was even more

95

beautiful than he could have imagined.

Bear's Paw and Nervous Woman pushed her gently toward the fire. The drumming grew faster until it matched the pounding of blood in Jesse's ears.

Morning Star began to sway back and forth in time to the rhythm. His mouth dried up as he watched her, and he only half-heard Cochise whisper: 'The smoke spirit is entering her soul, where it will eat up her old name so there is room for the new one.'

Abruptly the dance reached its climax. As the drums suddenly fell silent, so Morning Star gasped and then collapsed. When she failed to move again Jesse started to get up and go to her aid. Geronimo, his own movements as stiff as Jesse's, motioned for him to stay where he was.

Instead it was Cochise who rose to his feet and strode majestically toward the girl. He stood over her, raised his arms to the night sky and called: 'Hear me, Great Spirit! Morning Star is no more. In her place is this woman, known only by the name she has earned . . . Kin-say-oh.'

Sam saw Jesse frown, and leaned close to whisper: 'She-Who-Tames-The-Bear. It's fitting, don't you think?'

Jesse scowled. 'If you happen to like bears, maybe . . . which I don't.'

'So I've heard,' said Sam, trying not to grin.

'Good news travels fast,' Jesse growled, guessing the tale of his encounter with the bear had spread throughout the village.

At last Morning Star – now Kin-say-oh – climbed to her feet and Nervous Woman came forward to wrap her in the blanket. She smiled at the older woman and then searched the crowd until her eyes found Jesse. He winked at her and she smiled back at him. The smile warmed his belly.

*

Jesse awoke just after daylight next morning and found Cochise seated cross-legged before him.

Startled because he was a light sleeper, Jesse sat up and acknowledged the chief with a nod. ' 'Mornin'.'

Cochise said: 'The Council has made its decision.'

Jesse watched him carefully, but the chief's face betrayed nothing.

'The Chiricahuas will spill no blood for thirty sunsets,' Cochise continued after a pause. 'This will prove to your Great White Chief that the Apaches can live in peace.'

'What about Geronimo? Can he be trusted to keep that peace?'

'Geronimo was born a Bendonkohe, but he is a Chiricahua now,' Cochise replied simply. 'I am his chief. He will listen and obey.'

'That's good enough for me.'

'And let us hope it will also be good enough for your Great White Chief.'

Jesse gathered his gear together, then he and Cochise walked through the camp toward the remuda. 'I have arranged for one of my warriors to guide you out of the mountains,' Cochise said. 'And I will have my sentries keep watch for your return.'

'Thanks. I look forward to coming back.'

Cochise studied him closely. 'You think of Kin-say-oh when you say that?'

'She's one of the things I think of, yes.'

'Forget her, White-Eyes. There is no future for you and her together. She would miss the ways of her people, and you would become an outcast among your own, a squaw man.'

'It doesn't have to be like that.'

'No,' Cochise agreed sadly. 'And yet it *is*.'

He watched as Jesse saddled up, packed his gear and finally took back his weapons. Pausing, Jesse gazed about him but could not see Kin-say-oh. His heart sank and he prepared to mount up.

Cochise reached into his shirt and took out a folded square of buckskin. 'Here,' he said, passing it over. 'Take this with you. It shows what the Council has agreed and it carries my mark to prove that we are serious about this thing. Now ride to Fort Bowie and talk to your Great White Chief over the long-distance wires.'

Jesse reached down and offered his hand. Cochise shook it without hesitation. 'I will count the moons until you return,' he said.

'I'll be doin' the same thing,' Jesse said. '*Adios*.'

He nudged his horse forward and joined the awaiting guide.

As Cochise watched them go, Sam joined him.

'The fate of my people rides on this peace, *Haskiiyii-Thii*,' the Apache murmured softly.

Sam nodded, watching until Jesse and his guide were lost to sight. Peace. It should be so easy to achieve, and yet he was no more optimistic for its chances of success than Cochise.

CHAPTER EIGHTEEN

From high among the rocks, Geronimo also watched Jesse ride away. Then he descended to the camp below and went to find Kin-say-oh.

She was gathering firewood near the river. He watched as she tied her collection of kindling together with a rawhide thong and lifted the bundle onto her back. When she turned her mouth dropped open, because Geronimo, who had come upon her as silently as a thought, was standing in her way.

'Your white man has just left,' he said.

'He is not mine, Goyahkla,' she replied. 'He is just a friend.'

'Yet you cared enough for him to beg me for his life.'

'I begged for you to stop fighting each other,' she corrected. 'That is a different thing. In any case, I might just as well have begged him for your life. The fight was so evenly matched.'

He stiffened as if slapped. 'Geronimo needs no one to beg for him!'

Realizing this conversation was going nowhere, she said: 'May I pass now? Bear's Paw waits. . . .'

Geronimo stood his ground. 'Once, when we were children, you were not so anxious to pass. We were friends, then.'

'We were never friends, Goyahkla. You used to pull my hair and tease me, every chance you got.'

'Only because you ran from me.'

'And why did I run? Because you used to tease me . . . and hit me.'

'I did not hit you when Man-Who-Paints-The-Sky was killed,' he reminded softly.

'No. You were very kind to me then, and I will always be grateful to you for that. But you have changed – and more than just your name. You are full of hate now, Goyahkla, and it is difficult to like you.'

'It is hard not to hate when all you love is murdered before your eyes.'

'That was a terrible thing,' she agreed. 'When I was told about your wife and family, my heart bled stones for you. But you cannot blame all men for the actions of a few. If you do, your spirit will wither and the sun will never warm your heart—'

'*Kin-say-oh!*'

The sound of Nervous Woman's voice broke the moment. Kin-say-oh suddenly realized how close she and Geronimo had been standing, and stepped back just as Nervous Woman came around the bend in the trail.

'You would make Bear's Paw wait for his fire?' she demanded.

Kin-say-oh, once known as Morning Star, shook her head, and with a muttered apology edged around Geronimo and hurried on her way.

*

From behind his fastidiously neat desk, Major Calloway stared at Jesse with disbelief. 'You expect me to take the word of an *Apache*?'

Jesse had barely finished reporting the outcome of his peace mission when Calloway interrupted him. Biting his tongue, he threw a long-suffering glance at Lieutenant Travers and Ethan Patch, whom Calloway had called in, then said as patiently as he could: 'Not just any Apache, Major. The word of Cochise, the chief of the Chiricahuas.'

Calloway made a dismissive sound. 'Just because he's a chief doesn't make him any less of a liar,' he said stubbornly. 'All Apaches lie. Makes—'

'—people feel sorry for 'em. Yeah, that's what Calum Todd told me.'

Jesse suddenly fell silent, realizing he'd said the wrong thing. Now Calloway would tell him that Todd was dead, and that the girl he'd brought into Fort Bowie with him was suspected of his murder. But when the major said no such thing, Jesse continued: 'Well, I don't care what he or you or anyone else around here has to say about it, Major . . . I've got Cochise's word that there'll be no fighting or killin' or trouble of any kind for thirty days, and that's what I intend to tell the President.'

He turned to Patch, who'd been slowly chewing tobacco throughout the entire exchange. 'Ever seen Cochise's sign?' he asked.

The tall scout nodded. 'Once, yeah.'

'Then take a look at this.' He handed over the folded piece of buckskin Cochise had given him and waited patiently while the scout squinted at the pictures the Apache had drawn on it to depict the temporary truce. The signature was a drawing of an eagle holding an arrow in its talons.

'Cochise wrote it and signed it,' said Jesse. 'And as far as I'm concerned it's as fine a peace treaty as I've ever seen.'

Patch's nod sent a shiver through his shoulder-length blond hair. 'That's what it says right enough, Major. Never figured I'd live to see the day Cochise called a halt to robbin' and killin', not for any reason. But this seems to be it.'

Major Calloway looked disappointed. 'Well,' he said, 'if it's all the same to you, I prefer to reserve judgment.'

'I expect you do,' said Jesse. 'But a good general cares about the lives of his people, and he knows when to quit. And Cochise is a good general.'

'Very well. . . .' Calloway sniffed impatiently. 'But remember this, Glover. Thirty days is a long time. If your Apaches can restrain themselves for thirty *minutes* I'll consider it a minor miracle.'

Jesse clapped his hat on. 'Maybe you'd better reserve your judgment on *that*, too. Now, I'm headin' for the telegraph office so's I can pass this deal along to Washington. If the President accepts Cochise's terms, I'll expect you and your troopers to hold up the white man's end – even if it takes force to do it.'

Calloway flushed. 'You don't have to tell me my duty!'

'From where I'm standing,' Jesse said bluntly, 'someone sure does.'

Though Jesse was already heading for the door, Calloway had to have the last word. 'Well, when this treaty turns out to be a waste of time and lives, don't expect any sympathy from me, or from the ranchers or miners your Apache friends massacre! Because everyone around here knows that the only time we'll ever have peace with the Apaches is when they're all *dead*!'

The door slammed shut.

'That's tellin him, Major,' Patch growled.

The major wasn't sure if the scout meant it or was just being sarcastic. Before he could challenge him, Patch stomped out of the office.

CHAPTER NINETEEN

Jesse sent his wire and then wandered down to the trading post to find out what had happened to Calum Todd. He got the shock of his life when he saw the red-bearded Scotsman standing in front of the L-shaped log building, talking with four miners.

Kin-say-oh hadn't killed him after all!

Jesse felt almost light-headed with relief and ached to let her know. She'd certainly injured him, though; he wore a grimy bandage around his head and over his left ear.

As Jesse drew closer and Todd noticed him coming, the Indian agent's face darkened and he pulled the corncob pipe from his mouth with a white-knuckled fist. The four miners he'd been talking to saw the change in him and, their curiosity aroused, also turned to watch Jesse approach.

One of them, a short man in a threadbare brown jacket, rolled an unlit cigar from one side of his mouth to the other. The action woke a dim memory in Jesse – he'd seen the same man do the same thing the first time he'd met Ethan Patch down at the Ace High saloon.

'I dinna know how ye've got the nerve to show your face

around here, laddie,' Todd said as Jesse approached. 'That Apache bitch you foisted on me, d'ye ken what she did?'

'No. Tell me.'

'Bashed me over the head, she did,' Todd complained bitterly. 'Then stole my best horse an' lit out.'

'Really?' Jesse said innocently. 'Why'd she do that?'

'How do I know? She's just a savage, laddie, with a savage's nature. See the white man, *kill* the white man.'

'If she hit you over the head, Scotsman,' Jesse said, 'she had her reasons.'

'Oh? An' what would ye know about it?'

'Nothin',' Jesse replied. 'I just came down to see what had happened to the girl. Now I guess I know.'

As he turned and walked back toward town, Todd looked at his companions and said: 'Now, where was I? Och, yes. Come inside, laddies, an' have a wee drop o' the heather.'

The miners followed him into the dim store and at his invitation took seats around the makeshift barrel-table in the center of the floor. Todd produced a bottle of Old Overholt and four glasses. He poured shots and set them down before his guests. Then, taking the pipe from his mouth, he said: 'Lads, I'll be honest with ye – I've invited ye here today because we're facing what ye might call a mutual dilemma.'

The round-faced man chewed his unlit cigar across to the other side of his mouth. He was thirty but looked older. Like his companions, he was in need of a shave and cared little for his appearance. His name was Ben Kemp, and he'd been chasing the mother lode practically his entire life. 'What's that in plain talk?' he asked.

'In a word,' said Todd, 'Apaches. I've heard some very interestin' things around the fort today, boys. It seems there might well be peace in the offin' 'tween us an' the heathens. If it holds up, it'll put me under great scrutiny by the likes of that idiot Calloway . . . not to mention the Bureau of Indian Affairs.'

A tall man with a large nose gave a low, slow chuckle. Fair-haired and blue-eyed, this was Jim Landon. 'Meanin' you won' be able to cheat 'em out of their supplies no more?'

'An' sell everythin' on the side at triple the price,' added George Barker, who was bulky and bald as an egg.

Todd grinned. 'Laddie, I couldna have put it better myself. But it'll cut off *your* profits, too, don'tcha know.'

'How do you figure that?' asked Will Tucker, the fourth member of the group, licking the whiskey off the ends of his handlebar mustache.

'In exchange for peace,' said Todd, 'I hear that Cochise wants all minin' in Apache Hills to stop.'

He'd heard no such thing, of course, but he needed to lie in order to persuade these four to throw in with him.

Ben Kemp worried his cigar some more. 'Hell,' he breathed. 'He can't do that . . . can he? We jus' staked our damn' claim out there!'

'Yeah,' agreed Landon. 'An' we've found signs that look real good, like we might've struck pay dirt!'

'Too bad,' Todd goaded. 'If the treaty passes, you can kiss all that gold goodbye.'

'No damn Apache's gonna kick me off that claim,' Tucker grumbled.

'They won't have to, laddie. The military will do it for 'em. You lads ready to fight the United States Army?'

Their silence was answer enough.

'I didna think so,' he went on. 'Now do ye understand what I mean by a mutual dilemma?'

'What d'you suggest we do?' asked Kemp.

'Simple. Make the Apaches break the peace.'

'Oh? An' how we gonna do that?'

'Boys,' Todd said with a chuckle, 'I thought ye'd never ask. Now, listen up. I'm expectin' a delivery from Tucson a few days from now. To get here, it'll have to come through Apache Pass. Ye know the area?'

'Some,' Barker said.

'Good. Now, if the Apaches was to attack that wagon, burn it an' kill all but one of its crew. . . .'

'But how can we make the Apaches do that?'

'We can't,' said Todd, his eyes flattening. 'But you fellers can dress up like Apaches an' do it for 'em.'

Kemp stopped chewing on his unlit cigar. 'You mean murder our own kind?'

'That's one way of putting, laddie. I prefer to think of it as doing what we have to do to keep me in business an' you out there, workin' the mother lode.' He paused to let his words sink in, then said: 'Now – are ye in or no'?'

The miners glanced uneasily at each other. They didn't care for murder, but neither did they like being close to a fortune and having to give it up because some red savage said so.

'I don't like it,' said Kemp, looking at his companions. 'But . . . I reckon we're in.'

A grin split Todd's face. 'Good man,' he said. 'Now, here's the plan. . . .'

Leaving the trading post behind him, Jesse rode to the

tonsorial parlor on the next block and treated himself to a hot bath. It felt good to soak the trail dust out of his pores at last, and it also gave him a chance to think about Morning Star – Kin-say-oh, as she was now called. She was like no woman he'd ever known before. She knew her own mind, had courage to spare and there was absolutely no quit in her. But could Cochise have been right when he'd said there could be no future for them together? Hell, did she even want a future with him?

He dragged himself out of the tub, dried himself off and dressed in clean clothes. Then he entered the barbershop, sat in the chair and enjoyed the feel of a sharp razor scraping off his beard. A haircut finished the transformation, after which he went to find himself a meal.

He was halfway through a wedge of berry pie when the telegraph operator came into the restaurant, peered around through small, wire-framed spectacles and then, spotting him at a corner table, came over. He held out a flimsy sheet of yellow paper. 'Thought I might find you here,' he said. 'This came in about ten minutes ago.'

All at once Jesse's appetite left him. 'Thanks.'

He took the telegram, realized the operator was still loitering and shoved a dollar into his waiting palm. Then he unfolded the flimsy and quickly read it through.

AGREE TO COCHISE'S PEACE OFFER ON ONE CONDITION STOP ALL APACHES MUST MOVE ONTO RESERVATION STOP OTHERWISE NO DEAL STOP YOU HAVE SEVEN DAYS TO WORK OUT AGREEMENT WITH COCHISE STOP AFTER THAT MAJOR CALLOWAY IS AUTHORIZED TO USE APPRORIATE FORCE TO MAKE APACHES

GO ONTO RESERVATION STOP
PRESIDENT ULYSSES S GRANT

Jesse grimaced and balled the paper in his fist. To say he was disappointed was putting it mildly. As far as he was concerned, it just went to prove that even presidents weren't always as smart as they liked to believe.

He unfolded the page again and re-read it. Seven days. It sounded like a long time, but he had a feeling it wouldn't be anywhere near as long as it needed to be. He threw money onto the table for his meal, then left the café.

Next stop: Cochise's stronghold.

CHAPTER TWENTY

'Why should we accept your Great White Chief's conditions?' demanded Cochise.

Jesse had expected his reaction. It had been as predictable in its way as Calloway's, upon his return to Fort Bowie. "'Cause if you don't,' he said bluntly, 'soldiers will come and there'll be an all-out war – a war the white man will win simply because he is many and you're just a few.'

Cochise translated that for the benefit of the elders, whose knowledge of English was limited. They took it with stoic disappointment. Peace was one thing. That they could adapt to. But life on a white man's reservation? That was something else again. Most would rather die.

From his place in front of the Council lodge entrance, Geronimo watched the elders consider what Jesse had said. He didn't like what he read in their expressions. It was too much like defeat. Impulsively he yelled: 'Don't listen to him! It is better that we die in battle than live in defeat!'

Cochise stabbed a finger at him. 'You have no voice here, Goyahkla! Unless you wish to shame us further, say no more!'

Geronimo curled his lip. 'Why should I hold my tongue while old women decide the future of the Chiricahua? It is you who should feel shame!'

Behind him, the young braves who had gathered now muttered their agreement. Encouraged by their support, Geronimo added: 'I speak for all warriors when I say that we will never, ever live on a reservation! But know this, too, all of you! If we are to die, we will take many White-Eyes with us. This land will wash red with their blood!'

His message delivered, Geronimo stormed off. His supporters, fired up by such fighting talk, followed him.

Cochise sighed wearily and told Jesse: 'Forgive a young man his bad manners.'

'He knows how to get his point across, I'll grant him that.'

'He also speaks for the Chiricahuas. We will never agree to live behind fences, fed and clothed like helpless children by greedy men who would steal from us.'

'Then it looks like we've got ourselves a stand-off.'

Zulu Sam, who'd been watching the exchange from a few yards away, now came closer. 'OK if I say something?' he asked.

Cochise glanced at the elders, and when he received a nod of consent said: 'We will hear your words.'

'I've lived this life the whites are offerin',' he said. 'As a slave, I had no rights. I ate what they fed me, wore what they gave me, slept where they told me . . . and was whipped bad every time I tried to talk back.'

'No one's askin' the Apaches to be slaves,' Jesse said quickly.

'Ain't they?' countered Sam. 'You're takin' away their freedom, tellin' 'em how and where to live, makin' 'em dependent on you for just about everythin'. Maybe the wordin's different, but it still smells like slavery to me.'

Jesse turned to Cochise. 'Is that how you feel? That we're making slaves out of you?'

'You are a good man, White-Eyes, and I have learned to trust you. So I ask you: would you live this way?'

Jessc didn't even have to think about it. He shook his head.

'Well,' said Sam, 'at least you ain't no hypocrite. But he's right about one thing, Cochise. It's a fight you can't win, my brother. There are more whites than sand in the desert. They will send army after army at you. For every man you kill, three more will take his place. They'll wear you down and grind you under, eventually.'

'This I know,' Cochise said.

Sensing that this thing was going against him, Jesse said: 'Cochise, please think about it before you—'

'I *have* thought about it. And I have spoken about it to my people. They are prepared to die, if dying is the price we must pay for freedom.'

There was little to be gained by hanging around, so Jesse sought out Kin-say-oh and told her the news about Todd. Her relief was overshadowed by the news that had spread ahead of him: that war suddenly seemed likely between their two peoples.

'I wish it did not have to be this way,' she said.

'So do I, Kin-say-oh. But it is what it is. Rest of us just have to make the best of it.'

He was at the remuda, readying his sorrel for travel, when Sam found him. 'Think you can persuade the President to be reasonable?' asked the Zulu.

'Bein' reasonable ain't one of Mr Grant's strong points,' Jesse said. 'But he does want peace, so . . . maybe he'll listen. I'm not holding my breath, though.'

'The path of the peacemaker is never smooth,' quoted Sam. He looked quizzically at Jesse. 'You're kind of young to be playing peacemaker, anyway, ain't you?'

'Blame that on my pa.'

'The man Sittin' Bull took a shine to.'

'Wisest man he ever met, Pa said. He's your kind of man, Sam. Can talk to the spirit world, through animals, in his dreams.'

'Man listens, he'd be surprised what he can hear,' the Zulu said. 'Sometimes, at night, when I was alone in the desert with the mustangs, I swear I heard spirits talking to me.'

'What they tell you?'

Before Sam could reply, Geronimo confronted them. Behind him stood Blue Crow, Runs Slowly and Little Wolf.

Ignoring them, Sam said: 'That all men should be brothers and live in peace.'

Geronimo scowled. 'Peace only works for the white man.'

'That's where you're wrong,' said Jesse.

'Then prove it.'

'How am I supposed to do that?'

'You can't,' Geronimo said. 'There is no proving it.'

Behind him, his friends nodded.

It had been a long day and Jesse was short on temper. 'Your people an' mine will never get along until they start mixin',' he said. 'Think about it. You have your ideas about the whites. They have their ideas about you. Maybe it's about time we each started proving the other wrong.'

'I do not understand.'

'Ride into Fort Bowie with me,' Jesse said impulsively. 'See for yourself how safe it is.'

'And have the Long-Knives shoot me on sight?'

'No one's gonna shoot you, soldiers or civilians.'

'And if they try?'

'I'll shoot them first. And that's the end of *that* rope.'

Geronimo considered the proposition for a moment then looked at Sam. 'You believe this, *Haskiiyii-Thii*?'

'I don't know,' Sam replied honestly. 'But I'd be willin' to come along to find out.'

Geronimo studied both of them, eyes almost black in the sunlight. 'Then I shall do as you say, White-Eyes. It will be worth the risk just to prove you wrong.'

CHAPTER TWENTY-ONE

From their vantage point high in the rocks above Apache Pass, Ben Kemp and his three cronies watched a heavily loaded freight-wagon grind slowly along below them. Seated beside the man riding shotgun, the driver cracked his bullwhip high above the heads of his eight-mule team. Two more men, both mounted, flanked the wagon.

As he rolled his chewed, unlit cigar from one corner of his mouth to the other, Kemp tried to ignore his misgivings about what they were about to do. Calum Todd was right. If they sat back and did nothing, the army would boot them out of Apache Hills and they'd have to kiss all that sweet gold goodbye.

He couldn't let that happen. He'd been searching for color all his life, and had no doubt that there was money to be made from the claim they'd so recently staked.

No; it might not sit well with him to commit murder, but there wasn't much choice, not if he and his partners wanted to get rich – and they did.

He looked across at his companions. They, like him,

were dressed Apache-style in colorful shirts and loose-fitting pants tucked into knee-high moccasins. Todd had thought of everything – he'd even gotten them to crush berries and use the juice to darken their skin. He'd then told them to paint a stripe of white paint beneath their eyes and across their noses, just the way the Apaches did. He'd even supplied the black yarn from which they'd fashioned the crude, shoulder-length wigs that were now held in place by their makeshift headbands. The disguise might not be perfect, but it would pass in the heat of battle.

Still, Kemp was worried. They had the advantage of surprise, sure. But sooner or later those men down there would start shooting back. It was one thing to kill a man, he thought, and something else entirely to run risk of being the man who got killed.

Below them, the freight-wagon rumbled closer. It was a blue Conestoga with heavy red wheels, and had a grease-stained tarpaulin tied down tight over the supplies it carried.

Beside Kemp, Will Tucker fitted a home-made arrow to the string of the crude bow he'd constructed the day before. He'd also shaved off his handlebar mustache in order to pass for an Apache. 'Time to go play Injun, I reckon,' he said.

Kemp nodded. 'An' don't forget. Let the driver live, so he can tell everyone in Fort Bowie what happened.'

Together they pulled back from the ridge and mounted their ponies. Nothing had been left to chance; Apache blankets took the place of saddles and each horse was adorned with symbols: thunder stripes, red circles and palm-prints. Yessir, Calum Todd thought of everything.

Quietly they checked themselves over one last time.

The crack of the bullwhip, the rattle of chain and harness and creaking sideboards of the wagon all drifted up to them from below. Then George Barker looked at Kemp and slapped the ever-present cigar from between his lips. 'Where's your brains, Ben? Get rid of that thing or it'll give us away for sure!'

Kemp felt his temper flare but held it in check. George was right – it was a stupid mistake. He guessed his mind had been elsewhere.

They mounted up and quickly guided their horses down through a twisting rock-trail that brought them out to a covering spill of rocks just ahead of the freight wagon. The sounds were louder now, bouncing off the red-rock walls. One of the outriders had started singing *The Bronc That Wouldn't Bust.*

Lord, thought Kemp. *They don't suspect a thing.*

The first any of the wagon men knew about the attack was when an arrow flew out of nowhere and slammed through the singing outrider's neck. It choked the rider's voice off and, crumpling, he fell out of his saddle. On the other side of the wagon the second outrider immediately dragged his Spencer carbine from its sheath and yelled: 'Apaches!'

The driver started whipping the mules to greater speed, but the best they could manage was a fast trot. 'Up, mules! Hup! Hup! Yaaah! Yaaah!'

The blast of a rifle crackled along the canyon and the second outrider stood up in his stirrups, clutched his chest and then spilled head first to the canyon floor.

By now the wagon was rocking and bouncing. The guard brought up his shotgun – a hopelessly unsuitable weapon for this kind of encounter, but all he had – and

117

snap-aimed at the four Apaches who suddenly came charging out of the rocks. He pulled the trigger. One barrel blasted buckshot into the air but it was never going to hit anyone from this range.

One of the Apaches shot a flaming arrow at the wagon. It glanced off the sideboards and fell to the sand, where it quickly died out. The guard tried to stand up and face his attackers. He fired the second barrel and one of the Apaches fell from his horse, startled but otherwise unhurt.

The guard's moment of triumph was short-lived.

The next instant two fire-arrows struck him at the same time. He fell off the seat and down past the wagon-tongue. He was already dead and burning by the time he was crushed under the heavy wheels.

Moments later another fire-arrow found its mark. It slammed into the tarpaulin, which immediately started to burn. The driver stared back over one shoulder, his eyes wide and scared. His three companions had died in as many minutes and there was no reason to suspect he wouldn't be next.

God, I don't want to die. . . .

It was then that the wagon hit a rock and the rear axle snapped. Immediately he lost control of the wagon and did the only thing he could. He leapt off the seat even as the vehicle slammed against some more rocks and tipped over. Flames spread everywhere and dark smoke belched skyward.

The dazed driver staggered to his feet, sure now that his life could be measured in seconds. As he watched, the braves thrust their weapons toward the sky and started yipping like coyotes. But for some unknown reason the Apaches were holding back. Maybe they were waiting for their comrade to remount.

Still fearing for his life, the driver limped off into the rocks.

He couldn't believe his luck when, ten long minutes later, it finally dawned on him that the Apaches had let him go.

CHAPTER TWENTY-TWO

Although the folks who lived in and around Fort Bowie talked a lot about Apaches, it was only when Jesse rode down Main Street with Sam and Geronimo in tow that they realized how rarely it was that they ever actually saw one.

'They want to shoot me,' Geronimo hissed as he glanced from left to right. 'I can see the hatred in their eyes.'

'Easy, now,' said Jesse. 'They're just curious, is all. Remember how your people looked at me when you first brought me to the stronghold?'

Still, he couldn't deny that there was more hostility in the faces turned toward them than he would have expected, and he began to question his decision to bring Geronimo in.

Ahead, the fort drew closer, and Geronimo grew more and more uneasy. Even Sam started to look worried. 'You sure this is such a good idea, Glover?'

'Trust me,' was all Jesse said.

Word that they were coming spread ahead of them, so Jesse was hardly surprised when Major Calloway came hustling across the parade ground with Lieutenant Travers and Ethan Patch beside him.

'My God!' the major exclaimed as he saw them. 'It's true, then. Glover really has fetched the enemy to our door!'

'Got that right,' agreed Patch. 'You know who that there feller *is*?'

'An Apache,' Calloway said simply.

'Not just any Apache. That there is Geronimo hisself.'

Travers blanched. '*Geronimo?*'

'Shut up, you fool!' hissed Calloway. 'Once these people know who he is, there'll be a riot.'

But it was already too late. As Jesse and his companions reined up just inside the fort gateway he heard an ominous muttering behind him. Turning in his saddle he saw that a large number of townsfolk had followed them all the way down to the post.

What was worse, Geronimo's name was already spreading through the crowd. With it came a rush of old memories – how the Apaches had massacred some miners at Mill Creek, and burned the Wilson ranch to the ground, and murdered the Ford family over at Jessup's Crossing. There were fresher memories, too – like the way Hank Brownlow had stumbled into town the previous sundown to report that a bunch of Apaches had attacked his wagon and killed his three companions in Apache Pass.

A group of liquored-up townsmen burst out of the saloon, drew their sidearms and came charging down the street.

Too late Jesse realized he'd made a mistake in bringing Geronimo with him. But before any shooting could start, Major Calloway arrived with a squad of Springfield-toting troopers behind him. Never one to mince his words, he snapped: 'What the hell do you mean by bringing that savage here?'

Jesse said: 'I wanted to show him that the white man's peace works both ways. It *does*, doesn't it, Major?'

'I warned you once, Glover—'

Travers was watching the crowd. 'Better do something, Major, before we have a lynching on our hands.'

'Have the men keep the crowd back,' instructed Calloway.

Travers immediately started bellowing at the troopers. 'You heard the major! Form a line! Don't let anyone through!'

From the doorway of the trading post Calum Todd had seen Jesse and his friends arrive and couldn't believe his luck. Taking the pipe from his mouth he turned to Ben Kemp and the others and said: 'Played right into our hands! What did I tell ye? Brains and luck makes a winner out of a man every time!'

'Let's go down there,' said Landon. 'Stir things up?'

Not that they needed stirring. The scene around the gate was already ugly enough. But half-drunk as they'd been ever since ambushing the freight-wagon, Kemp and his friends thought it an excellent idea. Todd watched them stagger down toward the fort and grinned when he heard one of them cry: 'Got your soldiers protecting the wrong people, ain't ya, Major? Or have you turned Injun lover too!'

Calloway wheeled around and scanned the crowd until

he spotted the man. 'Don't tell me my job, mister!' he yelled back. 'Now, listen up, you people! This is an illegal gathering. Go on home, all of you. Go on!'

'Not till you give us Geronimo!' said Kemp.

The townsfolk started nodding. 'He's right! Better turn him over, Major!'

'Hang the murderin' bastard!'

'Yeah! Somebody get a rope!'

Urged on by the four miners the crowd surged forward, pushing the troopers back. Travers turned an agitated face toward the major. 'Sir, I think we're going to need more men.'

But Calloway drew his Colt and fired a shot into the air instead. Immediately it silenced the crowd and stopped them in their tracks.

'You have ten seconds to disperse!' he yelled. 'After that, I will instruct my men to open fire! Now, for the last time – go home!'

While they glanced at each other, waiting for someone to make a decision, Geronimo tightened his grip on his own rifle and, looking at Jesse, said: 'Where is your white man's peace now, White-Eyes?'

'Don't see those soldiers pointin' their guns at you, do you?' Jesse said.

George Barker called: 'What about it, Major? You gonna give us Geronimo or not?'

Jesse frowned at Calloway. 'What's wrong with these people, anyway?'

'They're fighting mad, Glover, and I can't say that I blame them.'

'Why? What's happened?'

'You mean you don't *know?*'

123

'How could I? I just rode into town.'

'Four Apaches attacked Calum Todd's freight wagon in Apache Pass yesterday morning. They killed three of the four men with it and burned the wagon!'

'He lies!' hissed Geronimo. 'No Chiricahua would break Cochise's peace! Not even Geronimo!'

'Well, there's your answer, Major.'

'I've seen the evidence,' Calloway said tightly. 'The bodies are at the undertakers – what's left of them.'

Again the angry crowd surged forward. Again Travers said desperately: 'Sir, we need more men!'

Calloway glared at Jesse. 'Perhaps I ought to just feed you to them after all!'

Jesse's hand dropped to his pistol. 'They might find us tough to chew on, Major.'

'All right – follow me!' He turned and led the trio across the parade ground – and then had them locked in the guardhouse.

CHAPTER TWENTY-THREE

Geronimo paced the tiny cell angrily, his hands flexing in rage.

From one of the bunks Jesse said: 'I'm telling you, this here's the safest place Calloway could've put us! Now, relax, will you? We'll all be out of here as soon as the major gets everyone calmed down. Then we can sort this thing out.'

'I wouldn't count on that,' said Ethan Patch, shuffling down the walkway fronting the cells.

Jesse came up fast. They'd been locked up for a little over three hours now, and it was starting to tell on all of them. 'What've you heard, Ethan?'

Patch's lined, lived-in face looked grim. 'Major's reached a decision. You boys showin' up here at jus' this time has really turned the town on its head. He's declared martial law till things quiet down. An' he's worked out a way to *quiet* it down, too.'

'They are going to hang us,' Geronimo said.

'Close enough,' Patch said. 'They're gonna hang you

an' your bare-chested friend here – but not you, Jesse.'

Zulu Sam took the news with a bitter twist of the lips. 'White man's justice,' he said.

'Wait a minute!' said Jesse. 'Why not me?'

'You're too well-connected, what with knowin' the President an' all.'

Before Jesse could reply Geronimo threw himself at him, slammed him against the bars and tried to choke him. 'You planned this all along, White-Eyes!'

Sam quickly dragged him off.

'Don't be crazy!' snapped Jesse. 'How the hell could I know any of this would happen? Anyway, fighting each other's not the answer. What's your take on it, Ethan?'

'It stinks,' the scout replied. 'Geronimo here's right. Ain't an Apache around who'd break Cochise's peace. 'Sides, that wagon contained all kind of supplies. You Apaches'd sooner loot it than burn it, am I right?'

Geronimo nodded.

'Any case,' Patch concluded, 'it all seems a mite . . . *convenient*. You know, three men die but these Apaches let the fourth get away, so's he can tell the tale?'

'Someone's tryin' to make sure there's no peace,' Sam said grimly.

'That's how I read it.'

'Who?'

'Ah, now there you got me,' said Patch. 'But someone who stands to gain from it.'

'Calloway?' asked Jesse. 'He's been spoiling for a fight ever since the Indians killed his brother.'

Patch shook his head. 'He hates the Indians, right enough. But I reckon you can rule him out.'

Jesse said: 'When's the hangin' supposed to take place?'

'Tomorrow noon. But I reckon you can leave 'most any time.'

'Then open this goddam door, Ethan! I want to see Calloway right *now*!'

Jesse came straight to the point. 'Major – you hang Geronimo or Zulu Sam and before you can spit you'll have a full-scale war on your hands.'

From the other side of his desk Major Calloway gave him a withering look. 'That's not your concern, mister. Your days as a peacemaker are over. You're leaving Fort Bowie immediately.'

'But—'

Calloway stood up fast. 'Read my lips, Glover. Show your face around here again and I'll find a reason to shoot you. Is that clear?'

'Real clear, Major.'

'Oh, and don't bother going to the telegraph office. It's off limits to you!'

Jesse's lips tightened. 'I'll be sure to tell that to the President . . . next time I wire him.'

'Please do,' returned Calloway. 'But I should warn you; when I informed President Grant about the Apaches breaking the peace, he authorized me *by return* to mount a campaign against Cochise and to keep at it until every single Chiricahua is either dead or on a reservation. Good day, Mr Glover.'

From the doorway of his trading post, Calum Todd watched Lieutenant Travers and four troopers escort Jesse as far as the town limits. When they reined up, Travers gestured with one gauntleted hand. 'Montana's that way, Glover.'

Jesse stared at him. 'You mean you ain't comin' with me? What a shame.'

'Don't take this out on me. For what it's worth, I agree with you – there's something about this entire business that's rotten to the core. But what can I do about it? I'm only a soldier. I can't have an opinion, I can only follow orders.'

'Travers,' said Jesse. '*Please*. You can't stand by and let Calloway hang two innocent men.'

'Then give me the guilty ones.'

'I aim to – though just how I'm gonna do it remains to be seen. Do me a favor?'

'If I can.'

'If I'm not back by tomorrow noon, do anythin' you can to stop that hangin'. If you don't, an' those two men die for a crime someone else committed, you'll regret it for the rest of your days.'

Travers looked grim. 'I can make no promises, Glover, but I'll do what I can.'

'Thanks.'

Jesse turned the sorrel and rode away.

He was certain the Apaches hadn't attacked the freight wagon crew. Cochise had given his word that they would keep the peace for thirty days, and, like Geronimo, he doubted that any Apache would dare to go against him. But if the Apaches were innocent, who was guilty?

All he knew right then was that he had to find out. The execution of Geronimo was just the spark the Apaches needed to go to war. That might oblige Major Calloway, but in the long run it would bring only suffering for white man and red alike. Besides, it was his fault that Geronimo and Sam were in this mess to begin with. Neither man would have come within a country mile of Fort Bowie if it hadn't been for him.

But even as he thought it, he realized it went deeper than that. He liked Sam. He was a good man. And if Geronimo hadn't been such a damn' hot-head, he had the feeling they could be friends, too. So he was going to do everything he could, because he sure as hell wasn't about to let those two end their days on a gallows.

In the guardhouse Geronimo and Sam were brooding over the way things had panned out. Outside, and still drunk, Ben Kemp and his cronies had come to taunt them, and though Geronimo and Sam tried to ignore them, it was hard.

'Just you wait till you feel the rope tightenin' around your heathen throats!' called Tucker.

'Comes time, it'll steal your breath away real slow,' added Barker. 'Gets so your tongue swells up so big it helps to choke you!'

'Body danglin' six feet off the ground,' Kemp jeered, 'all kickin' and chokin'. . . .'

'Don't pay 'em no mind,' Sam told Geronimo.

The Apache turned away from the bars he'd been gripping. 'Geronimo is not afraid to die. But this hanging . . . it is not a man's death.'

'Let's hope we never have to find out.'

Geronimo eyed him bleakly. 'We have a choice?'

'We might – if Jesse doesn't forget all about us.'

'He is free. Why should he care about us now?'

'I don't know. Hard to figure, I guess. But . . . I trust him, Goyahkla. I really do.'

CHAPTER
TWENTY-FOUR

Cochise knew something was wrong as soon as the three braves came galloping into the stronghold as if evil spirits were chasing them. He also knew it had something to do with Geronimo, for the braves in question – Runs Slowly, Blue Crow and Little Wolf – were Goyahkla's closest companions.

They drew their lathered ponies to a halt before Cochise's lodge and, exhausted, slid from their backs. The white man, Glover, had challenged Goyahkla to go with him to the Fort Bowie, Blue Crow told Cochise. He'd promised that Goyahkla would be safe, and Goyahkla had accepted the challenge to see how straight the white man's word really was. But, concerned for their friend, Blue Crow and the others had followed, keeping out of sight.

He then went on to describe what had happened at Fort Bowie, ending with Goyahkla and Zulu Sam being thrown in the white man's jail.

'For what cause?' Cochise demanded.

'No cause,' Blue Crow said. 'For just being an Apache.'

He added that according to the Navajos on the reservation all the White-Eyes were joking about it at the trading post. They were making bets on who would hang first.

'Chief Green Kettle says the man they know as Red Whiskers called it "white man's justice"!' said Runs Slowly.

'The White-Eyes have broken the peace!' Little Wolf said angrily. 'All Apaches must join together and wipe them out!'

The rest of the tribe gathered about them shouted in agreement.

'Wait!' Cochise said quickly. 'A wise man walks slowly into war. This could be the trick of a few white men, men who for their own selfish greed want to break the peace and give the soldiers a reason to massacre the Apache!'

'Even if this is true,' argued Blue Crow, 'Geronimo and *Haskiiyii-Thii* will still hang unless we break them out!'

'We must break them out!' declared Little Wolf. 'The time for talk is over! Give the word, Cochise! Call our people together and let us paint for war!'

The last word was drowned out by a roar of approval. Cochise looked into the faces around him. Men, women, young, old, even children – they were all stamping their feet in approval, their eyes shining with the prospect of finally ending this seemingly endless conflict one way or the other.

Reluctantly he said: 'It is agreed. Spread the message. Tomorrow we will attack the fort and save Geronimo and *Haskiiyii-Thii*!'

It was coming on dusk when the freckle-faced sentry with the almost invisible eyelashes thought he heard a noise off to his right. He turned and squinted through the gloom toward the guardhouse. There was no one over there that he could see, and now that he really strained his ears, all he could hear was the sounds of revelry drifting up from the Ace High saloon.

He guessed that the major had called it right. Promising to hang those two troublemakers had pacified the townsfolk. Tonight they were celebrating, looking forward to tomorrow's double hanging. The sentry wondered how he himself would face it. He'd never seen anyone hanged before, and even though it was an Indian and an Indian-lover who'd be dancing on air, it still didn't seem right him that it should be a cause for celebration.

Over in the corral behind the guardhouse, he heard the horses snort and whinny. The sound brought him back from his thoughts and he slowly wandered on.

Hunkered down behind a hollowed-out log water trough on the far side of the corral, Jesse waited until the sentry was out of sight and then ran to the guardhouse. He reached the wall, unseen, pressed his back to it and listened. No one raised the alarm. His eyes moved toward town. Someone was playing a merry tune on an upright piano. Men were laughing. He thought about the reason for their good mood and wondered who the real savages in all of this were.

A moment later he moved again, stopping only when he reached the barred window at the rear of the guardhouse. Peering inside, he saw Geronimo and Zulu Sam sitting on their bunks, each man alone with his thoughts.

He hissed and as they turned toward him, whispered: 'You two look so comfortable, maybe I should just leave you there.'

Instantly, Geronimo was at the bars. 'You came back,'

he said.

'Yeah, how about that?' said Jesse, feigning amazement. 'You surprised too, Sam?'

'I gave up bein' surprised by the white man a long time ago,' the Zulu said. 'Where you been, anyway?'

'Tryin' to prove it wasn't Apaches who attacked that freight wagon.'

'And?'

'I'll fill you in later. Right now, we got a hangman to cheat. Any ideas?'

'A diversion's always good,' Sam said.

'Reckon I could start a fire—'

'Horses,' said Geronimo, indicating the corral behind Jesse.

'What about 'em?'

Geronimo looked at Sam. 'If you were to talk to their spirits, make them run like their wild brothers. . . .'

Jesse stared at him as if he was loco, but Sam understood at once. 'Let 'em loose, Jesse,' he said urgently.

Jesse frowned. 'You're gonna talk to—' Then he remembered that the Apaches called Sam 'man-horse' for a reason. 'Anything else?'

'Uh-uh. Just hold two back for me an' Geronimo. I'll take care of the rest.'

Making sure he wasn't seen, Jesse crouch-ran back to the corral. When he reached it he opened the gate and then started working his way around to the rear of the pen. The horses shied away from him, nervous about this stranger whose scent was unfamiliar.

Just then someone in town fired his pistol in the air.

Jesse froze in his tracks, waiting.

But no one raised the alarm, and determinedly he

started herding the cavalry horses toward the gate, relying mostly on hand gestures for fear of alerting the sentries. At last, all but two horses were gone and Jesse quickly shut the gate before they could escape.

At the guardhouse window Sam began to make soft, gentle whinnies of sound that made the horses prick up their ears and stir restlessly. Beside him, Geronimo could only watch in wonder as the Zulu communicated with them.

Around the corner, in front of the row of low adobe buildings, the freckle-faced sentry heard the sound of horses moving around. He wondered what had spooked them. Maybe it was that damn liquored-up fool in town, shooting at the moon. He walked on a few paces.

Still he could hear the horses – and now that he thought about it, they sounded a whole lot closer than the corral.

On impulse he turned and went back to investigate.

At the same moment the horses came stampeding around the corner and across the parade ground.

With a yelp the startled sentry threw his carbine aside and dove for cover. Now all the sounds drifting in from town were drowned by the thunder of horses running in all directions.

Lights showed at windows. Doors opened. Major Calloway came racing out, pulling on his tunic, and pinned the shamefaced sentry with a glare. 'What the hell—? Don't just stand there, man! Help get those horses back!'

Jesse, meanwhile, had wasted no time. He led his sorrel across to the rear of the guardhouse and quickly tied a rope around the window bars. He then swung up into the saddle and tied the other end of the rope hard around the saddle horn. When he gave the horse his heels it lunged forward.

'*Yah! Yah!*'

The rope tightened like a bowstring, held taut for several seconds, and then, abruptly, the bars were yanked loose, tearing away part of the whitewashed adobe into which they'd been set.

Even as the bars broke away, Geronimo scrambled out through the window. Sam followed, cursing as he stumbled over the lumpy debris.

From there they ran to the corral and vaulted effortlessly onto the backs of the two remaining horses.

On the parade ground, officers and enlisted men alike had burst out of their quarters to watch the horses scattering. Some made half-hearted attempts at rounding them up. As Calloway bellowed orders, Lieutenant Travers happened to glance toward the corral, wondering how the animals had escaped in the first place. He was just in time to see Geronimo and Zulu Sam galloping toward the low wall spanning the rear of the fort.

He smiled as he recognized the third rider who joined them. Watching as the trio leaped over the wall and galloped unnoticed into the night Travers could not have been happier. Jesse Glover had just saved him from having to disobey the major's orders on the morrow.

CHAPTER TWENTY-FIVE

Jesse, Geronimo and Zulu Sam pushed their horses through the darkness as hard and as fast as they dared. Jesse led the way, blurring across shadowed plains until he was sure there was no danger of pursuit. Then the three men reined up and allowed their mounts to blow. Jesse passed his canteen around and, as the others drank, he fished out a litter of hand-rolled cigarette butts and a well-chewed cigar from one saddle-bag.

As he held them out for his companions to see, he said: 'I spent the afternoon lookin' around Apache Pass. I found the burned-out freight wagon and worked my way back from there. I'm not much of a hand with sign, but the sign out there was easy enough to follow. I traced it all the way back to where the "Apaches" killed time before the wagon came along. That's where I found these. And as we all know, Apaches don't smoke hand-rolled cigarettes.'

'Or cigars,' Sam said, adding: 'Why didn't you take 'em straight to Calloway, Jesse? They're evidence.'

'Sure they are. But they're nowhere near hard enough

evidence for *that* sonofabitch,' Jesse said grimly. 'That feller's set on hangin' you two no matter what. We're on our own from here on out.'

'I have smelled this before,' said Geronimo, examining the stogie. 'The men who taunted us about the hanging earlier today. One had this between his teeth – or one like it.'

'Lot of men smoke cigars,' Sam pointed out.

'Yeah. But this one hasn't been smoked, just chewed to death – and how many men do *that*?'

Sam frowned. 'Still ain't much to go on.'

'Unless you knew who chewed it.'

'Do you?' Geronimo asked.

'Think so. Before I broke you out of the stockade, I asked the barkeep at the Ace High saloon if *he* knew him, too.'

'And. . . ?'

'Said he'd bet his life it was a feller named Ben Kemp. When I asked him where I could find him, he said him and his three partners work a claim along Sage Creek.'

'I know where that is,' Sam said. 'It runs through Apache Hills.'

'Four men,' mused Geronimo. 'The same number who attacked the freight wagon.'

'Yeah,' Jesse said. 'Miners, too.'

'Does that mean somethin'?'

'It might. Morning Star – Kin-say-oh, I mean – told me that the Indian agent, Todd, sells supplies to the miners in Apache Hills – supplies that should be goin' to the Indians, who end up with next to nothing.' He thought a moment before adding: 'Coincidence?'

'One way to find out,' said Sam.

'Yeah.' Jesse grinned in the darkness. 'Let's go ask 'em.'

*

Dawn slowly illuminated two small tents pitched among scrub oak beside an unclean stream that wound through the rocky hills. Near by, a mine entrance had been blasted out of the hillside and a poorly constructed wooden sluice, supported by trestles, slanted all the way down to the water.

Still bleary-eyed from their late night celebrations with Calum Todd, Ben Kemp – for once minus his cigar – was dunking his head in the murky water to clear it. He could usually handle his drink, but he'd imbibed a little heavier than usual ever since Apache Pass. It helped to drown the voice of his nagging conscience.

Behind him, George Barker was fixing breakfast. It was the last thing Kemp needed right them – the smell of frying fatback was enough to make his stomach start churning all over again. But Barker had told him that a little grub would set him right, and he felt so fragile right about then that he'd agreed to give it a try.

Of course, there was some consolation in the fact that everything was working out exactly as Todd had said it would. Once the army cleaned the Apaches out of the hills, they could start blasting again and see just how much gold this vein really held. It was a prospect that filled all their minds.

'I hope them soldier boys do their job right smart,' said Landon, pouring coffee into an enamel mug. 'I ain't long on patience, me.'

'Todd says a few weeks at most,' said Tucker, idly feeling the skin below his nose, where his prize mustache used to be. 'Reckon the major's expectin' more cavalry an' extra howitzers to help blast Cochise out of his stronghold. I guess the President ain't long on patience, neither.'

The laughter died on their lips when a voice behind them said: 'That's 'cause he don't know all the facts.'

Before anyone could react, Jesse walked out of the brush fringing the rear of their camp.

'A mistake I aim to correct,' he continued. 'With your cooperation.'

Stunned, they recognized Jesse from their visit to Fort Bowie the day before. Tucker grabbed for the gun in his waistband.

Jesse was faster. His Peacemaker appeared in his hand, the muzzle moving slowly back and forth to keep them all covered.

'What the hell you talkin' about?' said Kemp, water trickling from his wet hair.

'I think you know,' Jesse said. 'But in case it's slipped your mind, my friends here are gonna help you remember.'

Geronimo and Sam stepped out of the trees and came to stand alongside him. Between his calloused palms Sam held the longest, thickest rattlesnake the miners had ever seen; their eyes bugged and their jaws dropped, especially those of Barker, who was deathly afraid of snakes.

'Wh-what're you aimin' to do with that sidewinder?' he stammered.

'Depends on you,' Jesse said. 'Tell the truth and Sam will hang onto that rattler. Lie to us and. . . .'

'. . . you'll all die curled up in agony,' added Sam. 'Kinda like men dancin' at the end of a rope. You remember – how it steals your breath away real slow, an' your tongue swells up so big it helps to choke you. . . .'

139

'All right, all right, we get your point,' Barker said. 'What d'you want us to say?'

'Shut up!' growled Landon.

'How it was you who attacked that freight wagon in Apache Pass,' Geronimo said.

'You're crazy!' Kemp said. 'We never attacked no—'

Sam took a step toward them, the snake giving a warning rattle.

'Easy, easy,' Jesse warned. 'You get that snake riled up an' maybe it'll slip out of Sam's hands and *bite* one of you boys. How about it?' he said as they recoiled. 'Memory comin' back yet?'

'We are wasting time,' Geronimo said. He pointed to Barker. 'Let me tie this one up and put the snake inside his shirt.'

Barker paled. 'No! W-wait . . . hold it . . . we was—'

Tucker suddenly made another grab for his pistol and this time it came out blasting.

Instinctively Jesse ducked and returned fire.

A red rose bloomed in the centre of Tucker's shirt. His eyes widened, he grunted and then collapsed into the brush behind him, legs kicking convulsively.

Landon dived into one of the two tents and grabbed a battered Winchester. Wasting no time, Jesse shot him. Landon doubled over and then buckled, taking the tent down with him.

Silence swallowed the sounds of violence.

'D-Don't kill me,' Barker said, cowering. 'Please. I'll tell you everythin'.'

'We're listenin',' Zulu Sam said.

Barker swallowed, hard, said: 'I was there.'

'Shut up, you damn' fool,' snapped Kemp.

'We all were,' said Barker.

'Dressed like Apaches?' asked Sam.

'Yeah. Warpaint an' everythin'.' He thumbed at the remaining tent. 'Our clothes'n stuff are in there.'

Geronimo hurried to the tent. After a moment of rummaging, he held up the crude wigs, a couple of colorful shirts, a pair of buckskin moccasins, the bows, the remaining arrows.

'Gents,' Jesse said grimly. 'I think we just struck paydirt!'

CHAPTER
TWENTY-SIX

As the sun climbed higher, Cochise's warriors prepared for war. They donned paint, decorated their ponies with protective symbols and collected their weapons. Excitement filled the air, especially around the younger braves. The older ones were more subdued as they bade farewell to their families and loved ones . . . perhaps for the last time.

Nervous Woman handed Bear's Paw his war-lance. Watching them, Kin-say-oh sensed that she was witnessing the end of her new life. She swallowed hard and went to turn away, but as she did so she saw Cochise striding across the encampment. He saw her at the same moment. Their gazes locked. Seeing the sadness in his eyes brought tears to hers.

Then he strode on. His own misgivings were as nothing when compared to the will of his people. They had set themselves for war and he could not stop them any more than he could keep the moon from rising. It was their choice, and he would lead them to their destiny . . . even if that destiny proved to be much different from what they expected, or hoped for.

At the fort, Major Calloway pulled on his starched white gauntlets and stepped up into the saddle, his 1861 model regulation cavalry saber slapping gently against his leg. When he was settled, he turned and surveyed the men behind him. They were standing beside the horses they'd eventually managed to round up again, each man's accoutrement-heavy McClellan saddle loaded down with everything he was likely to need for the campaign ahead. The sight filled him with pride.

At last he was about to embark upon the very course that up till now he'd only been able to dream about – the annihilation of the hated Apaches. And about time, too. How many men – good men, like his brother – had to die at the hands of the Indians before Washington finally said *enough* and allowed the army to do what it was meant to do?

Right now Glover, his friends and the Apaches were all laughing at him. But the laugh would be on them when Calloway launched his campaign on Cochise. They wouldn't be expecting *that*, and certainly not so soon. Until now Calloway's hands had been tied, and the Apaches had known it. But now the President had sliced through all that red tape and given him the orders to march.

Initially, of course, he had been prepared to await the arrival of additional troops and the promised howitzers. But the previous night's jailbreak had been the last straw. He had to act immediately and decisively – and so he would.

'Get the men mounted, Lieutenant,' he said quietly.

'Sir!' His expression unreadable, Travers saluted, then faced the men and yelled: 'Mount up!'

The order rang across the parade ground, and almost as one the troops swung up into leather.

Ethan Patch reluctantly did likewise.

'Column . . . right . . . wheel!' yelled Calloway. He held up his right hand, moving his fist in a tight circular motion with fore- and index fingers raised to denote that they should move out in columns of two. Then: '*Yo!*'

Calloway led the troop out of the fort, sitting tall and straight-backed in the saddle, a feeling of great pride surging through him. Both sides of Main Street were lined with townsfolk. The admiration he saw on their faces made his chest swell. These people had always considered him ineffectual. He knew it. What they'd never understood was that he was only following 'ineffectual' orders.

Well, from this day forward they were going to see a new side of Major Nicholas Calloway.

A woman in a gray dress and sunbonnet suddenly started clapping. He glanced at her, inclined his head and politely touched his fingers to the brim of his campaign hat. Then the man next to her joined in, and the people beside them. Soon everyone gathered along both sides of Main were clapping, whistling, cheering, and Calloway decided that there was never going to be a better moment in his life than this one.

Then Ethan Patch drew alongside him and spoiled everything.

'Major, for the last time I'm askin' you to call this foolishness off an' let me try an' talk to Cochise . . . try'n make some sense out of all this *non*sense.'

They'd been through this once already, and Calloway

144

was sick of the scout's attempts to undermine him. 'Absolutely not,' he snapped, hipping around angrily. 'Now, you have your orders, Mr Patch! You will lead us up and into the Dragoon Mountains or—'

'*Major!*'

Calloway hated to be interrupted. But there was something in Travers's tone that forced him to turn and look at the lieutenant.

Alarmed, Travers was pointing toward the open country beyond the town's limits.

Calloway squinted that way. 'My God. . . .' he muttered.

The Apaches had beaten them to it.

They were strung out in a ragged line along the ridge of the hills directly ahead of them, each silhouetted brave holding a rifle, a pistol or a lance over his head and screaming his war cry.

Calloway looked from left to right. How many were there – two hundred? *Three?* And how many men was he leading into battle? One company – eighty-two men.

Then the Apaches charged.

As they spilled down the distant, rock-strewn slope like a human waterfall, Calloway thought: *My God! He's coming for the town. Cochise is coming to wipe the town and the fort off the map.*

'Sir?'

He blinked at Travers, momentarily not seeing him. Then he yelled: 'Patch! Get these civilians off the street, now! Lieutenant, I want men deployed in every building and every rooftop along Main! We'll hit the Apaches from both sides the moment they enter town. Catch them in a crossfire!'

'Yessir!'

145

Behind Calloway the street became a riot of activity. Ignoring it, he took out his field glasses and raised them to his dark eyes. The Apaches were still a mile or so away; there was still time to prepare a warm welcome for them.

Then something else caught his attention.

Five riders were coming in from the east, cutting across the scrubland at an angle and galloping toward town. He squinted and screwed the eyepieces around to focus the field glasses more clearly. Then he swore. It was Glover . . . Geronimo and the Zulu he'd broken out of the guardhouse . . . and two other men the major had never seen before.

Jesse threw a look at the Apaches descending the distant blue slopes and his blood froze. Drawing rein he yelled: 'Dammit, we're too late!'

'No!' cried Geronimo. 'Go on to the white man's fort and tell them the truth of what happened at Apache Pass! I will turn my brothers back!'

'Can you *do* that?'

'Why do you think they are here, White-Eyes? They have come for *Haskiiyii-Thii* and me!'

'All right,' said Jesse, but Geronimo was already kicking his horse back to speed, sending it on a course across the flats that would intercept the lead riders.

'Sam?'

'Yo!'

Jesse looked from Kemp to Barker. 'Take our friends on into town.'

'What about you?'

'Know what happens when a ship starts to sink?' asked Jesse.

146

Sam thought about it. He carried a quiver filled with arrows across his back, and Will Tucker's home-made bow across the jute bag in his lap. 'The rats light out.'

'Uh-huh. Well, I'm gonna make sure that doesn't happen this time around.'

Sam's grin was fierce and cold. 'Good huntin',' he said. And then, to their prisoners: 'Giddap, there, you two! You've got some singin' to do to Major Calloway!'

Calloway had seen enough. He tucked the glasses away. As Travers came galloping back to report that the men had been deployed the major stabbed a finger at the oncoming trio. 'I want that criminal brought down, Lieutenant – now!'

Travers stared at Sam, who was walking his horse into town behind the two men with him. 'You mean . . . *shoot* him, sir?'

'Shoot him down like the dog he is, yes.'

'I can't do that, sir.'

Calloway glared at him. 'What?'

Swallowing hard, Travers said: 'In the first place, I won't shoot a man out of hand. In the second, for all we know he could be coming to help us.'

'Lieutenant, we were going to *hang* that man at noon today! Do you really think—' He bit off suddenly, fumbled with the flap of his holster and closed his hand around the butt of his Cavalry Colt. 'Never mind – I'll do the job myself!'

'But, sir—'

'And for disobeying a direct order, Lieutenant, consider yourself under arrest!'

Ethan Patch rode up, took in the situation and drew his

own Colt. 'Hold it, Major!'

Calloway looked at him, saw the gun pointed his belly and said: 'Damn you, Patch, how *dare* you raise a gun to me! I'll see you shot for this!'

'I wouldn't count on that, Major. 'Cause in two seconds I'm gonna blow a hole in your head to make room for some brains. Then, just for once, maybe you'll *listen* instead of running on pure hate . . . an' then this whole thing'll boil down to sense. Maybe.'

'But that man's an escaped prisoner!'

'So's Geronimo – but see what *he*'s doin'?'

Grudgingly Calloway looked. 'He's trying to get the attention of his heathen brothers!'

'Look again,' said Patch. 'He's *stoppin'* 'em.'

'He's right, sir,' said Travers.

Calloway looked, saw that the Apaches had slowed and were gathering around Geronimo.

By now Sam and the two men with him were within hailing distance of the town. The Zulu slowed his horse and signaled that he wanted to parley.

Patch yelled: 'It's all right! Come ahead!'

The three riders came on at a walk, even as the Apaches continued milling around on the desert, some of them already turning to head back for the hills.

When he was near enough, Sam reined up. Wordlessly he threw down the bow and emptied out the jute bag. A jumble of Apache clothes and wigs fell to the ground. The quiver full of home-made arrows followed seconds later.

'These here are Ben Kemp an' George Barker,' he said, indicating his unwilling companions. 'Two of the men who *really* attacked that freight wagon.'

Calloway's mouth thinned. 'I don't believe you.'

'Don't matter what you believe, Major. They've already confessed to their part in it and told us why they did it. They've even given us the name of the man who put 'em up to it. What more proof do you need before you'll admit that you've been duped?'

'There were four of them,' Calloway said stubbornly. 'Where are the other two?'

'Dead. Jesse Glover shot 'em in self-defense.'

Mind reeling, Calloway looked at the prisoners. Even he could see how guilty they looked.

'Who was behind it?' he demanded.

Sam grinned mirthlessly. 'I reckon Jesse's takin' care of *that* sonofabitch right this minute.'

They were halfway back to the fort when all hell broke loose.

CHAPTER TWENTY-SEVEN

Earlier, when word reached Calum Todd that Calloway was taking the fight to the Apaches, he poured himself a drink and toasted himself. The whole thing had gone down as smooth as sippin' whiskey. Of course, he'd known it would. That blowhard Calloway had always been champing at the bit to have a crack at the Indians. He, Todd, had merely given him the excuse he needed.

Yes, it had all gone down very smoothly indeed.

Until the Apaches had shown up.

Todd had been standing in the trading post doorway, watching Calloway and his toy soldiers trotting off to war when the major had suddenly registered shock and reined up. When Todd turned to see what he was looking at, his blood went cold.

He'd never thought the Indians would attack the fort.

His first thought was for his own skin. His second was for the safety of his store. Hurrying inside, corncob pipe still clamped between his teeth, he closed and bolted the shutters. Then he continued on to his quarters at the rear and pulled an old Remington pocket revolver from under his mattress. He was just about to return to the front of the store when he realized the window was open. He quickly yanked it shut and bolted the shutters over it.

He didn't notice the boot-print in the dust on the sill.

He ran back through the store, floorboards groaning underfoot, and came to a halt on the stoop.

In the distance the Indians had stopped their charge and were grouped around an Apache whom Todd recognized as Geronimo.

He cursed.

Worse, he now saw that Ben Kemp and George Barker were being herded into town by the big Zulu.

Todd slumped against the frame. He wondered what had gone wrong. It was a stupid question. He knew what had gone wrong. Somewhere along the way he'd underestimated that man Glover.

Again, he cursed under his breath. Only Kemp and Barker. What the devil had become of the other two? If they hadn't already done so, any one of the four would happily sell him out to make sure things went easier for them.

He was finished, then! All his future offered now was prison. Momentarily shaken by the prospect, he couldn't decide what to do. As Indian agent he had a nice little set-up here and it galled him to have to give it all up.

But did he have to? After all, all Kemp and the others could say was that they were carrying out his orders. But there was no written proof of that; it was strictly their word against his. And what jury with any sense would believe that a good, honest, hard-working Scotsman like Calum Todd would allow his own wagon and supplies to be burned black just to stir up trouble with the Apaches?

All at once he started to feel better about things. There was a chance of a way out of this yet.

Behind him, a floorboard creaked.

He spun around and saw Jesse standing beside the crude barrel-table.

They stared at each other for a long, tense moment. Then, 'It's over,' Jesse said grimly.

Todd frowned. 'Over, laddie? I dinna ken what ye're—'

'Save your breath,' Jesse said. He eyed the gun in the Scotsman's hand, adding: 'I'd sooner do this the easy way, Todd.'

'D-Do what?'

'Arrest you.'

Todd did his best to look baffled. '*Arrest* me? For what, may I ask?'

'Murder, attempted murder, incitin' a hanging, stealin' from the Indians. Do you want me to go on?'

Todd forced himself to chuckle. Sweat trickled from his temple down his jowl and on to soak into his red beard.

'Laddie, ye're barkin' at the moon. There's nary a word of proof in—' He jerked the Remington up and fired it at Jesse.

Jesse was already diving sideways. As he hit the floor, the bullet ripping splinters from the makeshift table, he drew his gun and fired. The shot was hasty. It missed Todd and thudded harmlessly into the log wall.

Todd fired again. The bullet ricocheted off the coffee grinder and hit the tree stump that served as a chopping block.

Jesse rolled over and scrambled up just as Todd fired a third shot. More by luck than skill, the bullet hit Jesse in the shoulder, slamming him back against the cracker barrel. The barrel went over, spilling crackers everywhere. Jesse followed it down, came to rest on his back, still as death.

Todd stared at Jesse with a gloating smile. His mind was already cooking up a rational reason to explain why he had killed him: Glover had broken into the store to make trouble. He, Todd, had tried to reason with him, but failed. They had argued and when Glover angrily started shooting, Todd had no choice but to defend himself. . . .

Jesse groaned.

Surprised, Todd stared down at him. He saw Jesse's eyelids flicker. Damn, the man was still alive! That meant another accusation he had to defend himself against.

Unless, of course, Jesse was dead.

Todd heard voices approaching outside. He had to act quickly.

He stood over Jesse, pointed the gun straight into Jesse's pale, drawn face and thumbed back the hammer.

Jesse looked up at him, eyes glazed with pain, knowing what was going to happen, knowing there wasn't a single damn thing he could do to stop it.

And then a guttural voice from the doorway behind Todd rasped: '*Yo, el hombre muerto!*'

Startled, Todd whirled around, saw an Apache – dammit, not just *an* Apache: that bastard Geronimo himself – and jerked his gun up.

Geronimo was faster.

He hurled the jawbone club he was holding and it spun end over end three times before its sharpened edge buried in Todd's bandaged forehead.

The Scotsman staggered backward, blood pouring

down between his wide, shocked eyes. His mouth gaped. The corncob pipe dropped to the floor and shattered. Then Todd collapsed, dead before he hit the boards.

It was over.

CHAPTER
TWENTY-EIGHT

When Jesse regained consciousness he realized he was lying on a bed in the Fort Bowie hospital. He was groggy and felt like hell.

'That'll be the ether,' the army doctor told him cheerfully. 'You'll start feeling better soon.'

Jesse nodded sleepily. 'Thanks, Doc.'

While he waited for the doctor's prediction to come true, he looked at the three visitors gathered around him.

Major Calloway said grudgingly: 'You and your, uh, friends here stopped a potential tragedy from happening today. For that you have my gratitude.' He coughed and cleared his throat. 'But I should tell you, Mr Glover, that that does not alter how I feel about you or Apaches in general or the men who consort with them.'

'I reckon that includes us,' Sam said, grinning at Patch.

Jesse eyed Calloway. 'It doesn't alter the way I feel about you either, Major. In my book: once an ass, always an ass.'

Then, as Calloway reddened: 'With your permission I'd like to use the telegraph. President Grant may not always be a reasonable man, but he knows how to deal with the truth.'

Calloway fumed silently, then said: 'Permission granted. And when you've sent your wire, you can get the hell out of my fort.' He marched to the door, opened it and looked back. 'Oh, and Mr Patch. . . ?'

The tall, grizzled scout used his tongue to shift his chew to the other cheek before saying: 'I know, Major. I'm fired.'

'As of right now!'

Patch grinned. 'Why, thank you kindly, sir. Reckon you're finally startin' to make some sense . . . you sorry, sanctimonious sonofabitch.'

Much later, when they were back in Cochise's stronghold, Geronimo said: 'I still say it is a mistake for the Chiricahuas to trust the white man's offer of peace.'

'Only time will tell, *hermano*,' Sam said.

'Time's what the President's given us,' Jesse reminded. 'Who knows, maybe with enough time we'll be able to work out something agreeable yet.'

It was the best they could hope for, and after all they'd been through it was enough.

'You are ready?' Cochise asked them.

They looked at each other, then nodded.

'Then let us join your blood.'

He led them to the fire that was burning in the center of a cleared area, thrust the blade of his bone-handled knife into the flames and waited for it to heat.

Geronimo looked mockingly at Jesse. 'Are you not afraid of mixing your blood with mine, *indaa*?'

Jesse shrugged. 'I'm willin' to live dangerously. How

about you?'

'To a Chiricahua, there is no other life.'

'What about you, Sam?'

'I'll risk it,' Sam said.

At last Cochise pulled the knife from the fire. The blade glowed red and a thin trail of smoke wormed toward the sky. 'Extend your left arms.'

They did so.

Very deliberately, Cochise cut each man on the wrist, drawing blood. Then Jesse and Geronimo ceremonially pressed their wrists together on the cut and held them there for a moment. Both then did the same thing with Zulu Sam, all deliberately rubbing their wrists together to make sure the blood mingled.

'It is done,' said Cochise. 'What blood has joined, no man can part.'

As Jesse wrapped a kerchief around his wrist, he said: 'If you will permit it, Cochise, I need to speak to someone.'

Cochise smiled faintly and nodded. 'Do what you must do, my friend.'

Jesse hurried down to the stream, hoping to find Kin-say-oh there. When she was nowhere to be seen he was more disappointed than he could have imagined. But his disappointment was short-lived. Her voice suddenly called to him from the nearby oak trees.

Turning, he saw her step out into the sunshine. In a dyed-white doeskin dress adorned with red, blue and green beads, and a rawhide thong holding back her long black hair, she looked so beautiful that Jesse could only stare at her.

'How did you know I would be here?' she asked, joining him.

157

'I didn't,' he managed to say. 'I just hoped.'

'It is rude, of course, to ask a direct question, but. . . .'

'Ask anyway.'

'Would I be wrong if I thought you were not disappointed?'

'With what?'

'The way Nervous Woman has dressed me?'

He laughed. 'How could I be? When I saw you a moment ago, your beauty drained all the strength from my legs.'

She looked away, embarrassed.

'Does that please you?'

'I am not permitted to say.'

'You more than please me,' Jesse said. 'I want to spend the rest of my life with—'

She stopped him, visibly troubled by his words. 'Where are your blood brothers?' she asked.

'With Cochise.' He smiled and took her hands in his. 'It's not Apache law that we have to be together every second, you know.'

'I think at least one of your brothers would disagree,' Kin-say-oh said.

Jesse heard a noise behind him. Turning, he saw that it was Geronimo.

'Leave us,' he told Jesse. 'I wish to speak to the woman alone.'

'Well, there's a coincidence,' said Jesse. 'So do I.'

Ignoring him, Geronimo pinned Kin-say-oh with a baleful stare and said: 'It is time you took a husband. I will speak with Bear's Paw. Ask him how many ponies he wants for you.'

'You will do no such thing.'

'Music to my ears,' said Jesse, grinning. 'I don't have any ponies to offer, Kin-say-oh, but—'

'Stop it!' she interrupted. 'I do not want to hear what you're going to say. I am no horse to be bought or traded for. Nor am I ready to marry anyone!'

'But just now I thought. . . .'

'If you wish to wait until I am ready,' she continued, 'that is fine. But until that day, all we can be is friends.'

Geronimo crossed his arms defiantly. 'And if I, Goyahkla, do not agree to this?'

'Or me,' Jesse added quickly.

Kin-say-oh shrugged and whistled softly.

A moment later her guardian, the huge black bear, Little One, lumbered out of the trees. Raising up onto its hind legs, paws extended, teeth bared, it gave a warning growl.

Jesse blanched.

Beside him, Geronimo gulped.

'Come to think of it,' Jesse said. 'I can wait.'

Geronimo ignored him. His eyes never left the giant bear.

Slowly, reluctantly, both men backed away from the girl they loved.

'At last,' Geronimo said to Jesse. 'We agree upon something.'